ALBERT HAGERTHY

PHAETON 309

SOLAR FLARE CHANGES HEART

Hagerthy, Albert
Phaeton 309, Solar Flare Changes Heart

Albert Hagerthy
p. 156
1. FICTION / Science Fiction / Apocalyptic & Post-Apocalyptic
2. FICTION / Science Fiction / General
I. Title

ISBN: 979-8-8691-2900-0

Published by
Old Trucker Books
Woolwich, Maine

Printed in the United States of America

Dedicated to my wife Michelle and the families
of those who struggle with transplant complications.
You are my inspiration.

Chapter 1

June 12 at 3:14 PM, Route 1, South Portland, Maine

A red and white 1989 Ford F350 pickup drove north on Route 1 in South Portland. It passed by Rudy's diner on the left then over a bridge above railroad tracks and down a small incline to a traffic light. The pick-up turned right at the light onto Dartmouth Street continuing until it came to the O'Hegerty Trucking driveway, where it turned left into the office parking lot. The truck proceeded into the space marked Driver of the Year. The pick-up driver hopped out, grabbed his lunchbox from the passenger seat. Closing the driver's door, he glanced at the F350 International logo on the front fender. The man looked at the O'Hegerty trailer lot, where four reefer trailers were parked. He turned, walked toward the office building, and opened the drivers' room door.

Three men were talking in the driver's room. The tallest one looked at the man entering the room and said, "Hey Paul, great timing. We are going to the Can Afford warehouse for a meeting with Ron LaFlute. He has some big announcements about the future of all their trucking. I think you should come along. You know more about how their trucking schedules work than anyone here."

"Ok, how long will it take? My first trip leaves at 4:00 PM," Paul said.

Donald replied, "When I talked to Ron this morning, he said it would be a short meeting."

Bob said, "Was he talking about himself or the meeting?" They all laughed, and Bob continued, "Well, if we go there now, Paul can leave on time for his first trip."

They all nodded their heads. Paul spoke as they walked out the door where Paul entered, "As long as Ron doesn't get into one of his long short stories."

"Yeah, he's good for rambling on," Donald said, shaking his head.

Bob said, "It's a nice day. Let's walk over." They all agreed. They walked down the steps by the red O'Hegerty tractors, then past the trailers and dock doors at P.R.C. They made it to the street and walked across it to the Can Afford employee parking lot.

As it left the warehouse, an International Lonestar stopped at the security gate. Mark pointed and asked, "Paul, what do you think of that truck?"

Paul replied, "It kinda reminds me of the Jaguar S-type commercial, something old and something new."

"Yeah, that's a good comparison. I like it. I'll get with Wayne at PENSWAY Truck Leasing after July 4th to see what he thinks about them," said Mark.

They made it through the parking lot to the security rotary personnel gate. Donald swiped his security pass and went through the rotary gate.

Bob was next as Mark checked his pockets and said, "Damn it, I left mine on my desk."

Paul handed his pass to Mark and said, "Here use mine then hand it back to me so I get through."

Mark asked, "You sure?"

Donald said, "It doesn't matter who uses the card as long as it's not damaged the computer system will let you in."

Mark said, "Ok," then moved through the rotary gate and handed the pass back to Paul. Paul swiped and walked through. They all walked across the warehouse paved yard to the security office and warehouse employee entrance. A security guard sitting in the security office looked up with a half-smile and said, "Hi."

Donald swiped his security pass then opened the glass door and all four men walked through to a wide hallway lined with pictures of Can Afford's trucks of the past.

Donald opened the metal door on the left for the stairs leading to the second floor. They open the door at the top of the stairs to a lobby that separated Can Affords' dispatch from the administration offices. Truckin Bob and Ken Hews came from dispatch into the administration area at the same time.

"Hey, the gangs all here," joked Truckin Bob.

Donald asked, "Do you know anything about the 'big announcement'."

Truckin Bob replied, "No, Ron and corporate have kept it a secret."

"Ron loves this control of a secret. Just makes himself feel big," said Bob.

Ken said, "You got that right." They all laugh a little.

Bob said, "Ron wants to use the bigger corporate meeting room at the other end.

Mark said, "The one with a stage?"

"He wouldn't have it any other way." Bob said and they laugh again as they walk past all the offices to the auditorium.

A person stood at the podium testing the microphone. Truckin Bob led the men to the front row. Donald walked to a seat in the second row from the stage. Bob, Mark, and Paul followed and sat down. Truckin Bob and Ken sat in front of them, then the warehouse department heads walked in and sat in the third row.

The corporate heads from the main office in Scarborough are the last to walk in. Ron walked in with them. Together they walked to the front row and sat down. All except the corporate president, Anthony Fitzgerald who walked up to the podium, grabbed the microphone, and began speaking, "Good afternoon. On behalf of Can Afford, thank you all for your dedication to keeping this corporate machine running. With several VPs, Ron LaFlute and I, he pointed toward Ron, have had some intense meetings regarding how to improve trucking to its best potential. We agreed.

"Ron, you should come up and explain the plan since this is your field of expertise." As Ron stood up with a self-satisfied grin on his face, Truckin Bob turned his face (with a look of horror) to Donald, Bob, Mark, and Paul. They all had smirks on their faces trying not to laugh.

Ron moved to the podium, picked up the microphone, brought it to his mouth and said, "Thank you, Anthony."

"Welcome all of you today to this special announcement. I with Mr. Fitzgerald and all of Can Afford corporate have perfected a plan to be the number one leader in grocery store deliveries in New England."

Kenny Hews softly coughed to clear his throat.

Ron continued speaking, "Can Afford corporate has purchased several new tractors with state-of-the-art computer software. For the best fuel economy and satellite tracking. So, we can perfect the PM grocery deliveries, transition the tractors and trailers back to the warehouse to reload the morning produce, meat and dairy. Now with our goal of being number one there will be a greater demand for our drivers to be at their peak performance. During a dozen meetings over the last year, we went through statistics on the abilities of younger drivers versus older drivers. We made a calculated decision regarding Can Afford senior drivers, they will be given an generous early retirement severance package. As for our contract transportation drivers that are sixty years and older, your services will no longer be needed."

Truckin Bob had a perplexed pissed-off look on his face. Truckin Bob stood up then Mark O'Hegerty joined him. Bob said, "Now wait a minute, Can Afford's best drivers are the senior drivers as well as Mark's drivers. You can't just toss them out like yesterday's newspaper. They are the ones that got us where we are today."

Bob Tyghman stood and said, "That's right," Bob extended his hand pointing at Paul, "Paul has never refused to haul a load for Can Afford no matter what the weather."

The Can Afford president scurried to the podium and took the microphone, "I, Ron, and all the VPs have had these discussions. With no bias towards older drivers, we decided it would be safer all around by giving the senior drivers an early retirement. Can Afford's senior drivers and Mark, your senior drivers, deserve to retire with their physical health still intact. The Can Afford administration and I would not be able to forgive ourselves if one of those senior drivers got physically hurt and could not enjoy their retirement. This was the way the Can Afford founders would have wanted it."

CHAPTER 2

June 26 at 11:00 AM, *Ruby's Diner, South Portland, Maine*

Two weeks later, Paul arrived at the dinner and took off his faded O'Hegerty trucking hat. He placed it on the counter as he sat on a stool. On the other side of the counter, a woman in her fifties put a coffee cup in front of Paul and poured some into the cup. As the cup filled, she said, "Paul, you're coming in late this morning. Don't tell me you were out looking for a part-time driving job."

Paul replied, "No."

The waitress continued, "Then what, recuperating from a hot date last night?"

Paul replied again, "No, I was at Maine Med checking in on Albert's wife."

The waitress asked, "Not cancer again."

Paul replied, "No, remember when she had that defibrillator put in because the chemo treatment damaged her heart?"

The waitress has a concerned look on her face. She said, "Oh my God, that was years ago. Is she all right?"

Paul said, "Yes and no. She's in the ICU at Maine Med, hooked up to a lot of heart-controlling equipment. Albert was there, and he said that the Boston heart doctor had put Michelle on the heart transplant list. Now they have to wait for a donor."

The waitress groans, "How long of a wait will that be? And can she hold on that long?"

"I asked Albert the same question and he said they don't know how long the wait will be. Then he said the heart machines will keep her alive as long as needed."

The waitress asked, "Was she awake?"

"Yeah, she was in and out because of the meds. They said she would be fully awake in the late afternoon."

"I'll have to visit and give them both some encouragement," the waitress said.

"I told Albert she has a much better chance at living a long life, unlike my wife." Just then, the front door opened and three Can Afford drivers and Ron LaFlute the head of Can Afford trucking enter.

The waitress whispered, "Oh God, not that pompous ass."

Paul replied, "Watch it, he's got short man syndrome."

"His height isn't the only thing he has shortness in," quipped the waitress and they laughed together.

Ron looked down the counter and saw Paul and the waitress. "Hey, follow me." With a swagger, Ron led the men over to Paul. Paul was taking a sip of his black coffee lifting the mug with his right hand.

Ron approached Paul putting his left hand on Paul's right shoulder with enough pressure to cause Paul to spill coffee on his face and shirt. Paul grabbed some napkins to clean his face and shirt.

Ron said, "I'm sorry Paul did I do that? How have you been? Are you enjoying your retirement?"

"I was until you came in."

Ron didn't acknowledge Paul's reply and continued speaking, "Hey, these are the first three drivers that are going to deliver to Can Afford stores with the new Automatic Tractors. All the new Can Afford drivers will now be able to out do any of your best delivery times."

Paul and the waitress looked at each other. She rolled her eyes. Paul said, "I'll be right here to watch them on the maiden voyage." The waitress and Paul continued looking at each other.

The waitress asked Ron and the three drivers, "Can I get you men anything?"

Ron jerked his head a little as if to come back to the real world. Ron said, "Oh yes, Jenny, I'm buying these drivers lunch before they go out on their maiden voyage." With an arrogant smirk on his face, he nudged Paul's right shoulder again.

Jenny took the lunch orders from the three drivers and then Ron's order. She handed the four lunch orders to the cook. Then Jenny turned and asked Ron and the three drivers, "Where are you going to sit?" Ron looked at the clock on the wall and said, "Damn, can we have that to go? We have to meet with the President of Can Afford before they leave on their trips."

Paul said, "Yeah, you better hurry up. You might be meeting with an empty chair."

Jenny told the cook, "Those orders are to go."

The cook replied, "Yup."

While Ron and the three drivers waited for their lunches, Ron discussed with them what to say to the president of Can Afford.

"Order up!" The cook then handed the lunches to Jenny

and she placed them on the counter. Ron and the drivers grabbed their lunches. They start walking to the front door.

Ron stopped, looked at the receipts with Rudy's Diner's logo and telephone number, he said "Jenny I got your number for a good time…meal. I will put it on the wall at Can Afford dispatch." Ron turned and raised his voice, "Hey, Paul, in about an hour the maiden voyage will drive by, don't miss it."

Paul replied, "I will be right here,"

As Ron and the three drivers left the diner, Jenny grabbed a coffee pot and poured coffee for Paul. Jenny shook her head, while rolling her eyes and with an annoyed tone, "He is such an ass. Now you know, if I had known yesterday, he was coming in today. I would have made him some double fudge ex-lax brownies and put some in with his lunch."

Paul grinned, "That would be a good idea. I can imagine him not even being able to run fast enough to make it to the bathroom in time. What a big stink that would be!"

Jenny and Paul burst into laughter.

An hour went by, and Jenny looked out the window, down the street to the traffic light and saw the new trucks waiting for the light to change. "Hey, Paul, the trucks are at the light."

Paul stood up to look out the window, picking up his hat and cup of coffee, thanking Jenny, he walked out the front door. Jenny followed Paul. They both go outside to get a better view of the traffic lights. As they looked on, a new Chevy Pickup truck headed up the street toward them, followed by three Maroon Volvo automatic transmission tractors pulling Can Afford trailers. Just as the pickup made it to the diner, Paul and Jenny saw Ron driving. Ron tooted the horn and waved his right hand like a beauty queen at a pageant. Paul took a sip of his coffee.

Then Jenny said, "Do you think he will ever wake up someday and realize he has been a complete ass all his life?"

Paul replied in a confident tone, "What goes around, comes around. Whether or not he wakes up will be a different story, but I doubt it."

Paul took another sip of coffee and watched as the three new trucks drove by. Paul raised his cup in validation to the last driver as he drove by. The three drivers waved to Paul and Jenny.

Paul and Jenny headed back into the diner. Paul ate lunch and waited for Jenny to finish her shift. After Jenny clocked out for the day, they both departed in their separate vehicles and headed to Maine Med to visit Albert and Michelle.

Upon arrival at Maine Med, Paul and Jenny walked together through the hospital doors. Once inside Jenny took a moment and glanced around the lobby area and said in a surprised tone, "Geez, this place looks busy today." Paul and Jenny navigated their way through the chaotic surroundings and to the ICU. When they arrived at the nurses' station, Albert was leaving Michelle's room to get some coffee. He saw Paul and Jenny.

Albert greeted them, "Michelle will be happy to see you both."

Jenny asked hopefully, "Is she awake?"

"Yes, she has been awake for about an hour now."

Meanwhile Paul asked the nurse if it was ok to visit Michelle, making sure that they would not intrude on her need for rest.

The nurse stated, "Yes, you both will be fine visiting her, she seems to feel a little better today."

Paul smiled and thanked the nurse. Then Paul, Jenny, and Albert walked toward Michelle's room.

As they entered the room, they noticed Michelle was channel surfing through the TV. With heightened emotion Jenny asked, "How do you feel?"

There was a brief hesitation then Paul chimed in, "What are you looking for on TV?"

Michelle said, "I was hoping they would have AMC so I can watch The Walking Dead."

Paul looked at Albert, shook his head and said, "Only Michelle." They all laughed.

Jenny looked around and down the hallway by Michelle's hospital room, "Where are Marc and Felicia? How are they holding up?"

Albert answered, "Marc is in the cafeteria," Michelle added, "Where else would he be?" They all chuckled.

Michelle continued speaking, "Felicia was visiting her friend, Kayla, in Washington State. They are both trying to get a flight back here tomorrow."

Jenny offered, "I will pick them up from the airport. Just let me know when and where."

Michelle smiled and gave an appreciative look, "Thank you so much, and could you write down your phone number on a piece of paper, so Albert can contact you with their flight information?"

Jenny nodded and wrote down her number and handed it to Michelle.

They both glanced at each other, and Michelle stated, "You

know Albert, if it's not written down, he'll forget it."

Jenny said, "Oh yes, men would be lost without us," with a smirk.

Michelle nodded her head and then continued, "I will admit, Albert being a small-town hick from Maine, he does know his way around the streets of Boston like the back of his hand."

As Michelle and Jenny continued with their conversation Paul and Albert discussed other matters.

Paul asked Albert, "Has anyone from O'Hegerty called you yet, wanting to know when you're coming back to work?"

Albert replied, "Yeah, Donny did." Paul made a face while rolling his eyes, "But he asked how Michelle was doing first."

Paul raised his right eyebrow, "That was nice of him."

Albert then said, "I told him it may be a week, maybe more. No one knows yet. I said I would keep him informed."

There was a short silence and then Jenny stood up, "Well, Paul, we should go so Michelle can rest."

Paul nodded and replied, "Yes, so she can watch 'The Walking Dead'."

Jenny backhandedly smacks Paul on his shoulder.

Paul looked back at Jenny and asked, "What? That's the show she was channel surfing for when we got here."

Jenny ignored Paul's comment and walked over to Michelle's bedside and took Michelle's right hand. Jenny told Michelle, "I'll be back tomorrow after I get out of work. Let me know about Felicia and her friend, and if you need anything else."

Michelle nodded her head and Jenny continued, "Hang in there I have my hands full with Paul."

Michelle smiled, “I will, besides, Albert will become a hoarding hermit without me,” they both chuckled.

Paul began to speak with Albert and said, “I’ll see you both tomorrow. Don’t worry about Donny, I’ll talk to him. Before we leave, we will check on Marc for you. Get some rest.”

Paul and Jenny headed for the door saying in unison, “See you tomorrow!” and walked out of the I.C.U.

CHAPTER 3

July 3 at 3:14 PM, Can Afford's Warehouse, South Portland, Maine.

It was early Monday morning before two at Can Afford's warehouse. Loaded over the road, trailer trucks lined the dimly lit street approaching the warehouse. Each truck driver began checking in at the main gate to be assigned a dock door to back into or where to park on the hill. Over the road drivers waited for the next available dock door in a large parking lot inside and to the right of the main gate. Five O'Hegerty drivers pre-tripped their tractors and started the engines. At the same time, Four Can Afford drivers arrived and started their assigned tractors. All nine drivers left PENSWAY, truck leasing fleet maintenance company, tractor parking lot. Then they drove through the main gate of the Can Afford warehouse. Two O'Hegerty drivers went to an empty trailer parking lot across from the freezer. They hooked up to the two empty O'Hegerty trailers. Both trucks left the Can Afford Warehouse yard and began their trip to the Boston produce market. The other three O'Hegerty drivers and the four Can Afford drivers parked their tractors in parking spaces near the Can Afford dispatch office. All seven drivers went into the warehouse, passing the outside smoking area.

The seven drivers went upstairs to the dispatch office to collect the paperwork needed for their trips. During the drivers' walk from the tractors to the warehouse, the Can Afford drivers commented about the brand-new Volvo automatic transmission tractors they would drive. They all said that they loved driving them. They bragged about how all they would have to do was steer and that the computers in the tractors did all the shifting for them.

The O'Hegerty driver's tractors are 10-speed manual shift transmissions. Two of those three O'Hegerty tractors are three-year-old Volvos, and the last tractor was a W900 2001 Kenworth. Two Can Afford drivers asked Albert, the O'Hegerty driver with the Kenworth, when Mark would get rid of that old junk truck.

Albert, employee #509, said, "I'd rather drive that old Kenworth than a computerized truck. I don't need a computer to tell me how to drive. Besides that, Kenworth can out pull any of those automatic transmission tractors."

All four Can Afford drivers laughed, "Yeah, right..."

The other two O'Hegerty drivers remained silent. But they shook their heads with distrust for a computerized shifting truck.

As the drivers started up the stairs to dispatch, the Can Afford driver, who had called the Kenworth an "old junk," continued to boast. The driver said, "With this new Volvo, I'll finish my trip faster and get an early start on our family 4th of July cookout."

The dispatch room was an open cubicle with three computers and Bob. Bob was the Can Afford dispatcher. All the Can Afford drivers called him "Truckin Bob." Off to the right of the dispatch cubical area was a long table. Several paper-clipped load diagrams with computer printout sheets for each store delivery were spread out on top of the table. At the far end of the table was another computer and a copier machine. The computer was for the Can Afford drivers to log into the system to leave with their assigned trips. As the four Can Afford drivers started logging into the computer, the O'Hegerty drivers grabbed their given load diagram sheets and headed over to Bob and told him the load numbers they were taking. Bob then handed each O'Hegerty driver another trip sheet and logged all three O'Hegerty drivers into his computer.

Now back to the Can Afford drivers...they are having some trouble logging into the driver's computer, which was linked to their new tractors' computers. Bob's computer also manages their driver's logbook. The O'Hegerty drivers leave dispatch to return to their tractors. They start their tractors to go around the warehouse to pick up their assigned trailers.

The O'Hegerty drivers hooked up to their trailers, closed the trailer doors, and put padlocks on the right door. Then they got inside the tractors and updated their paper, handwritten logbooks...no computer needed. All three O'Hegerty drivers drove out through the main gate. Albert, driver #509, was the last of the three O'Hegerty drivers to leave. As he turned left to go through the gate, Albert saw the four Can Afford drivers coming out of the dispatch door. Albert mutters, "Great computer system."

After Truckin Bob managed to get the four Can Afford drivers logged into the computer, he called the tech support office in South Carolina. As he explained to the tech support what was happening with the drivers logging in, Bob commented,

"You know we didn't have this much trouble until Del Hayes made us tie completely into their global system. Is there something wrong with the satellite dishes in space?"

The tech supporter snapped, "NO! You and your drivers are not used to Del Hayes's highly advanced computer system."

Bob said, "OK...can you do a complete diagnostic analysis of the drivers' logins and logouts within the past 24 hours?" Just as Bob was going to finish his request, five more drivers entered the dispatch room, four O'Hegerty drivers. Along with one Can Afford driver returning from Schodack, N.Y., the location of another Can Afford Warehouse Distribution Center.

Bob looked at the drivers and finished speaking to the tech. "Five drivers just came into dispatch, I've got to go, but can you get back to me before seven this morning with what you found?"

The tech replied, "Yes, I will try." Bob thanked the tech and hung up the phone.

Bob immediately spoke to the Can Afford driver, Rick (he looked like ZZ Top). "Hey Rick, are drivers in Schodack having trouble logging in and out of the Zaida computer in dispatch?"

Rick replied with an annoyed, "Yes."

Bob hesitated for a few seconds, then continued talking to the Can Afford driver. "Hey, let me get these O'Hegerty drivers their trip sheets so they can get going. Then I'll help you log out so you can go home."

The Can Afford driver replied with a short "Yup."

Bob asked each O'Hegerty driver what their trip numbers were. Bob gave the O'Hegerty drivers the paperwork for each load.

During this time, Albert's truck sat second in line at Pensway's Fuel Island to fuel up the reefer trailer he's hauling. Albert turned on the AM/FM radio to listen to Coast to Coast with George Norai. George was speaking to Richard C. Hoaglen "guest speaker". They were discussing breaking news in the science community.

Richard said, "The Sun was experiencing some huge solar flares. Scientists are predicting serious effects on Earth and the satellites in space between Earth and the sun when any highly electrically charged waves from these solar flares reach Earth. All satellites in space between the Earth and the sun will have their computers wiped out."

George asked, "Can scientists monitoring these solar flares predict when the waves will reach Earth? Also, will anything on Earth be affected?"

"Yes, they can predict the impact time to the outer atmosphere. Now I just got to say, not knowing the strength of these waves, they can push those satellites into the Earth's Ionosphere, causing them to crash into the planet. Plus, damaging communication in the Ionosphere." As Richard finishes this sentence, Albert drove up to the Fuel Island as the driver ahead of him drove away from the fuel pump.

Albert shut off the tractor's engine after he set the parking brake. The Pensway's Fuel Island attendant, Steve, was getting onto the catwalk on Albert's tractor, platform space behind the cab, to check the engine oil level to the reefer unit of the trailer. As Steve did this, he asked Albert how things were going.

Albert replied, "Right out straight and crazy as always during a big holiday. But it sounds like things are going to get worse."

Steve asked, "How's that?"

Albert answered, "This scientist was just talking on the radio about gigantic solar flares sending electricity-charged shock waves to Earth. When these shock waves get here, a bunch of satellites out in space will be damaged, and some might crash to Earth."

"Oh great, we get to have more fireworks," said Steve as he finished fueling the trailer, "You are all set, Albert, have a safe trip, and watch out for the satellite fireworks."

Albert started the engine, released the parking brake, and then drove out of the fuel Island to begin his trip. As Albert went by the main entrance to the Can Afford warehouse, he looked at the line of over-the-road drivers waiting their turn to deliver their loads to the warehouse. Albert lets off the throttle to look at those computerized plastic junks Can Afford drivers have. Then Albert stepped back on the throttle and continued driving. He comes to a traffic light, and several gas tanker drivers pass. Albert turned up the volume on the AM/FM radio, the clock time was 3:09 AM, and the light turned green.

Albert turned left to go South on Rt. 1 and drove uphill onto the bridge that crosses over the South Portland Railyard tracks. He passed by Rudy's Diner and, farther down the street, saw Dunkin Donuts on the right. One of the O'Hegerty drivers with a Volvo tractor (new last year) was parked on the right.

The O'Hegerty driver walked with his coffee, looking down the street, and saw Albert getting closer. The driver said to himself, "Oh no, he's not getting ahead of me." The driver ran to the truck, hopped in, spilled some of the coffee, "Shit."

He released the parking brake, put the manual transmission into gear, and pulled out into the street ahead of Albert.

Albert slowed down but blew out a deep sign.

They both continued to the next traffic light, where they needed to turn right. The Volvo stopped and then turned to the right onto a four-lane throughway to the Maine Turnpike. The Volvo driver stayed in the right lane. Albert followed, then moved into the left lane to pass the Volvo.

The Volvo driver looked at his left door mirror and saw Albert gaining on him in the left lane. The Volvo driver increased his speed so Albert could not pass him. Albert stepped on it and passed the Volvo.

Albert reached for the CB mic and asked the Volvo driver, "When will you learn? Ken Worthington trucks are the king of the road."

"Ya ya ya," the Volvo driver grunts. "Tell that to the Can Afford drivers." Albert replied, "I did, and they laughed. After all, their computerized trucks are the best of the best. Just ask them. Are you going to the produce market after your last store?" The Volvo driver replied, "Ya, are you?" Albert replied, "Yes, and I'll try to get there before you so you can take the watermelon load, and I can take the lightweight State Garden." The Volvo driver replied, "You better not. Well, have a safe trip anyway, and I see you down there."

Now Albert and the Volvo driver entered the Maine Turnpike and headed South. Albert continued to listen to "Coast to Coast."

"Out in space, this electricity-charged wave was making its way toward Earth. Space particles are being pushed and collected to follow the path of the huge tsunami wave of power."

CHAPTER 4

July 3 at 3:00 AM, NASA, Florida

At NASA, in Florida, space agency scientists were scrambling and calling other space agencies around the planet. They were working on computer models to predict the timing of the wave hitting Earth. The International Space Station needed to be moved into lower orbit and behind the Earth. Arecibo in Puerto Rico was measuring the speed of the wave. The Arecibo scientists detected a slowdown as the wave gathers space debris and wind. This slowdown could take a little time to determine whether to speed up or slow down the space station's orbital speed. The space station occupants were getting very anxious.

July 3 at 5 AM, Lowell, Massachusetts

Albert left Rt. 495 South at exit 38 Lowell, Mass., then turned right at the end of the off-ramp, drove a short way, and stopped at a traffic light. When the light turned green, Albert turned left onto a smaller street, then a quick right, and went behind a McDonald's. He turned left again to go behind the Can Afford grocery store.

Three vendor trucks are parked at the grocery dock. Albert passed the trailer grocery dock, then backed into the dock. Albert walked around to the grocery vendor dock. As he walked up the ramp, he heard one of the sales vendors complaining that the inventory computer in his truck wasn't working right. Albert pushed the receiving doorbell and waited for the door to open. The vendor continued to complain. Just as Albert shook his head, the door opened, and the store receiver let him in.

Albert told the receiver, "You have fourteen pallets, and I'm going to the produce market, so no clean out."

The receiver asked Albert, "Are any other drivers coming by to take the dunnage?"

"I don't know, you will have to call Can Afford Dispatch, but I wouldn't do that right now."

The receiver asked, "Why?"

"When I was getting the paperwork for this load, Bob in dispatch was having a lot of trouble with the main computer."

Then Albert and the receiver started unloading the fourteen pallets. Thirty minutes later, Albert walked out onto the vendor dock to go to the last store. The vendor who was complaining about his computer was hand counting and writing down the inventory numbers on a piece of cardboard. Just as Albert walked by the vendor, he looked at Albert.

The vendor said, "I will be here all day at this rate." Albert shook his head again and continued walking to the truck.

The sun was at the horizon. Albert returned to the truck and drove to the Dracut, Mass Can Afford store.

After Albert backed into the dock and walked around to the vendor dock, he heard some vendor salespeople complaining that their computers were not working right. Albert continued walking to the grocery receiving door. The receiver was operating a fork truck, moving Coke pallets down from the storage rack to the grocery backroom floor. As he placed a soda pallet on the floor, the receiver asked, "How many pallets?"

Albert replied, "Fourteen," Albert opened the dock door, rolled up the trailer door, and then pushed the button for the dock plate to go into the trailer.

The receiver got off the fork truck, went to the receiving desk, and used the phone to access the intercom system, "Produce trucks here." The receiver returned to the fork truck and drove into the trailer as Albert stood beside the dock plate.

Thirty minutes later, Albert used the same phone at the receiving desk to call O'Hegerty dispatch to let them know that he was leaving Dracut, Mass, and on his way to the produce market. The dispatcher replied and tells Albert, "Don't stop anywhere and get to the produce market as soon as you can. Troy's pulling his hair out; he only has two other drivers helping him." Albert replied, "Alright, I'll call you when I'm loaded and ready to return to Maine."

Albert walked outside onto the vendor dock. One of the vendors stood in the back of his delivery truck, yelling, "What a piece of shit I can't get any inventory."

Albert continued to walk to the truck, got in the cab, and updated his logbook. He started the Kenworth, then drove out to the street and turned right, then East onto Rt. 113 toward Rt. 93. Both sides of the street were lined with American flags waving slightly in the breeze from light posts.

Traffic picked up as Albert got closer to Rt. 93. Albert drove South on Rt. 93 and in the middle lane because traffic flows faster. As Albert continued driving South, he looked to the

Northbound lanes and saw three Grocery Basket trailer trucks, older Mack tractors, driving North to New Hampshire.

Albert continued South on 93 during this time, his radio was tuned to FM 105.7 WROR, "Men from Maine Story." Albert passed four Lillie's Market tractor trailers (older Volvo tractors) driving Southbound. Albert moved to the right middle lane to avoid on and off-ramp traffic. Now after the Stoneham exit, traffic slowed down to 10 mph. (6:45 AM)

Back in South Portland, Maine, Truckin Bob was pulling out what was left of his hair. Can Afford drivers called in on their cell phones and told Bob that their trucks would not start. Some of the drivers were trying to leave the dock at stores. A lot of drivers were driving on the highway. Some are on streets in the middle of busy traffic light intersections. Some are going through Turnpike Toll Booths.

Now all the incoming call lights were lit up on Bob's phone. Bob looked up and saw two guys from Load-Con walk by to get coffee in the driver's room.

Bob called, "Hey, can you two help me with these incoming calls? I have to call the Pensway tractor shop because I got a bunch of Can Afford drivers with their trucks broken down."

Both men went to the other phones in the dispatch area and started to answer the incoming calls. Some drivers were a bit upset and raised their voices at the Load-Con guys. The Load-Con guys started writing information down on who and where they are. Bob called the Pensway tractor shop to inform them of this chaos.

Larry answered the phone at the Pensway tractor shop, "Pensway services."

Bob said, "Hey, Larry, this is Truckin Bob at Can Afford,"

"Yes, Bob, I already have a service truck on the way to Cash Corner."

"It's not just that truck; I think it's all the Can Afford trucks."

Larry said, "What do you mean?"

"Larry, all the Can Afford drivers are calling in, saying their trucks won't start. A lot of them were driving, and the engines just shut off. What the hell is going on?"

Larry responded, "I don't know. Let me call the mechanic at Cash Corner to see what he has found out, and I will call you right back."

"Ok, make it fast because this is really bad."

"Bob, I know, give me five minutes."

Larry called the mechanic at Cash Corner. He parked the service truck in the middle of the Intersection beside the Can Afford trailer truck. A South Portland police officer was trying to direct traffic around the disabled truck.

The mechanic was plugging his diagnostic computer into the truck computer, and his cell phone rang. The mechanic answered, "Yeah?"

Larry said, "Hey Steve, have you found out anything yet?"

"No, GIVE ME a minute. I just got it plugged in."

As the mechanic was searching through the software, Larry said, "Truckin Bob from Can Afford just called and said all the Can Afford trucks are broken down."

Mechanic said, "Really?!" Just then, the diagnostic computer screen started flashing, and the anti-theft security lock was flashing. The mechanic continued, "It's the anti-theft security lock."

Larry said, "Oh shit, we don't have the code to clear that.

Try disconnecting the battery, and I'll call Bob for the codes."

Larry called Bob, and Bob answered the phone, "Can Afford Trucking." Larry said, "Bob, it's Larry. The mechanic said the anti-theft security lock shut down the engine. I need the codes to unlock it."

Bob said, "What? I wouldn't have that. Del Hayes set that system up. I will have to call them in South Carolina for that information." Bob hesitated to speak, rubbing his forehead with his left hand. Bob continued, "Larry, I'll call Del Hayes to get the codes. I don't know how soon I'll call you back." Larry responded, "Ok."

Bob hung up the phone--annoyed, frustrated. Now Ron LaFlute, the head of Can Afford Trucking, had just arrived at the dispatch office. Ron was just about to ask Bob what was going on.

Bob speaks first, "I don't know yet. I just got off the phone with Larry at Pensway. He said the mechanic at Cash Corner told him the anti-theft security lock system that Del Hayes set up in all the trucks shut down the engines, and he needs the security codes to unlock the computer in the trucks."

Ron asked, "Why? Hasn't anyone called for the codes yet?"

Bob replied, "I was going to call just as you came in." Bob held the phone in his hand. Ron stood in dispatch with an impatient semi-panic look watching Bob dial the phone number. Bob put the phone to his right ear, looked at Ron, and then said, "I shouldn't have to make this call because the administrator in charge of trucking should already have these damn codes."

Both Load-con people on the other phones stopped what they are doing with an 'Oh shit' look on their faces.

Bob spoke into the phone, "Hello, this is Truckin Bob in South Portland," Bob paused to listen to a recording.

"Hello, you have reached Del Hayes Corporation. Due to the heavy call volume, your call will be answered in the order it was received. Please remain on the line. Your call is very important to us."

"Really?" Bob muttered. Then Bob handed the phone to Ron and told him, "You wait for someone to talk to. I have to call Pensway." Bob walked into Karen's office and used the phone to call Larry at Pensway.

Larry answered the phone, "Pensway Service."

Bob said, "Larry, it's Truckin Bob. I can't get the codes right now. Ron LaFlute is on hold with Del Hayes, but he could be on hold all day."

Larry said, "What do you mean? Or why?"

Bob said, "Well, if this security lock has stopped the Can Afford trucks, it may have stopped all the other trucking companies Del Hayes owns."

"Wow!" Larry exclaimed.

Bob said, "I'm not waiting for the codes. We need to get the trucks blocking roadways moved first. Can you get the one moved from Cash Corner?"

Larry said, "I'll call Stewarts right now, but I'm going to need to know where all the other trucks are."

Bob said, "I got Load-Con getting the location of the other trucks; we need to get the trucks blocking intersections first. Hopefully, by then, we will have the codes. You need to get the one at Cash Corner first, call Stewarts, then I'll call you back with the location of the other ones." Bob hung up, left Karen's office, and looked at Ron.

Bob said, "Ron, anything?"

Ron looked up as he was sitting at the dispatch counter with a wrinkled forehead, phone held to the left side of his head. Ron shook his head. "No."

Bob acknowledged and walked over to the load-con guys. Bob said, "I need the locations of all the trucks you have so far." Just as Bob finished speaking, Karen walked around the corner to enter her office. Bob quickly looked toward Karen. Bob said, "Karen, I need you to go through the locations of all these trucks."

Karen said, "What's going on?"

"All of the Can Afford trucks have stopped because of the anti-theft system that Del Hayes installed and has shut them all down."

Karen said, "I wonder if the solar flare has anything to do with this?" Ron said, "I bet it does."

Bob said, "What solar flare?"

Karen said, "It's all over the news. Satellites in space will be damaged, and cell phone communication may stop. Even electric power grids may shut down."

Bob said, "Oh, that's just lovely." Bob continued, "Karen, I need the trucks blocking major intersections first, then the trucks on roads, streets, and highways in that order, and the trucks at stores we will deal with after."

Bob handed the truck location papers to Karen; Ron started to get up and head towards Karen. Bob began to walk out of dispatch to go to the bathroom. He came to a quick stop with a slight body turn to the left, at the same time raising his left arm and pointing his pointer finger at Ron. Bob said, "No, you stay on the phone. Karen doesn't need your help."

July 3 at 6:55 AM, O'Hegerty Trucking office,

Donald walked in the door by the driver's room. The night dispatcher, Rick, said, "Oh, thank God you're here; the phone has been going crazy."

Donald said, "Is it because of the traffic jam on Rt. 1?"

Rick said, "No, I don't think so, maybe."

Donald said, "Well, what is it?"

Rick said, "You know that GPS system Mark put in the six Volvo tractors?" Donald said, "Yeah."

Rick continued, "Well, all six tractors have shut down and won't start." Donald said, "Does Pensway know?"

Rick replied, "Yes, Larry said all of the Can Afford tractors have done the same thing, and he has a mechanic at Cash Corner trying to move a Can Afford driver's truck."

Donald speaks, "That's why I had to come in the back way because the traffic is all backed up. Anyway, where are the six tractors?"

Rick replied, "One is at the Allston toll booth on the Mass Pike on his way to Quincy. One is in the Peabody, Mass Can Afford store parking lot. Two are on 95 South in New Hampshire. One is at the dock at JFK Plaza in Waterville. The last one is at the Cottage Road Can Afford store at the dock also.

Donald said, "The two in Mass and the two in New Hampshire, are they scheduled for the market?"

Rick said, "Yes."

The phone rang. Rick answered the phone, "O'Hegerty Trucking."

Troy spoke through clinched teeth, "What the fuck is going on? I got 20 loads to get out of here and only 5 drivers. I need help down here."

Rick replied, "Albert is on his way from Dracut."

Troy said, "Who else?"

Rick replied, "Well, you did have four other drivers, but their trucks are broken down."

Troy said, "Great! I need five more drivers. I don't care who; just get them here."

Rick said, "I'll tell Donald."

Troy said, "I need them here no later than 10:30 this morning. Tell Donald I'll call him back in thirty minutes." Rick replied, "Ok."

Now in the small office of 4M Fruits Building, Troy hung up the phone, all pissed off. Gonzo (an O'Hegerty Trucking produce market driver "cattle farmer") looked at Troy, and Gonzo said, "What now?"

Troy explained, "Four trucks have broken down. Donald has to get replacements. I don't know who or when. So, we have to get these loads ready ourselves; where is the State Garden load?"

Gonzo replied, "Outback."

Troy said, "If you see Albert before I do, tell him to drop his empty trailer at Arrow and take the State Garden load." A brief hesitation, "Oh, also, he may have to do a double because he's the only driver that won't stop."

Gonzo replied, "Aah, ya mean you can't."

"Yeah."

July 3, at 7:00 AM, Route 93 Southbound, Medford, Mass.

Albert exited Route 93 South onto Route 16 East headed to the produce market. Albert reached with his left hand to the lower left side of the dashboard and turned on the engine clutch fan. Now he stopped at the second traffic light in the right lane of a three-lane road. The traffic light turned green, and intimidation began. With the clutch fan on, Albert can shift the transmission much faster. When the engine revs up, it sounds and feels like a freight train hell-bent for election.

During this 1.5 to 2-mile ride to the produce market, three cars tried to cut in front of Albert at different times, but only one made it. The other two didn't because Albert wouldn't let them. During this 1.5 to 2 miles, a MTA Bus passed in the right lane #1309. Albert reached the produce market and pulled into 4 M's street-side dock area. He saw Gonzo hooking up to a Can Afford trailer at the street dock. Albert pulled the parking brake, quickly exited the truck, and then walked over to Gonzo.

As Gonzo hooked up the airlines to the trailer, Albert said, "Where's Troy?"

"Troy said to drop your trailer at Arrow and pick up 8079 from here. State Garden load. Make it fast because you're probably doing a second load."

"Why?" Albert asked.

Gonzo replied, "Four trucks broke down, and we don't know who or even if there will be anyone to replace them. So, get going." Albert ran back to the truck.

CHAPTER 5

July 3 at 4:30 AM, Arecibo Observatory

Three Arecibo Observatory scientists reported their findings to NASA engineers. Arecibo described the scenario of its best guess of where and when the wave would hit Earth. NASA scientists contacted other space agencies around the planet sharing this information. Foreign space agencies replied with the same and or nearly the same information.

Once notified, NASA, Russian, Canadian, Japanese, and the European space agencies worked together to find the best location for the space station to ride out the wave of the effect of the solar flare. NASA contacted the space station with this information and agreed upon coordinates to avoid or at least minimize any damage from the surge of the solar flare. The space station astronauts began to bring the station closer to the Earth.

July 3 at 8:00 AM, Rudy's Diner, South Portland, Maine

At Rudy's Diner truck stop, Paul Garrish, a retired O'Hegerty driver, was sitting at the counter eating breakfast. Diesel, the retired Can Afford yard jockey and driver, entered the diner and saw Paul.

Diesel said, "Well, Paul, you were right. All that technology has failed. How will the great Del Hayes Corporation deliver to all those stores?'

Paul said, "You could pull a couple of loads for them with your little cabover and make it back in time to pull your granddaughter's Girl Scout float in the parade.

Diesel replied, "Ya, but one of the reasons I retired was because the administration said we were getting too old and too slow. Del Hayes's new fast-paced system would be too much for us. We would be more like debt than profit." Paul said, "If they don't make up their minds fast, there won't be any profit."

Kenny Hews, the day dispatcher for Can Afford, opened the diner's front door. "I knew you two would be here to watch the new tractors fail."

Diesel said, "We're here for a great breakfast. We'll stay for lunch if Del Hayes keeps up with this free entertainment." Diesel pointed at the large flat-screen television showing Stewards pulling the Can Afford tractor-trailer from the Cash Corner intersection.

Kenny said, "Hey, Paul, you still got your old car?" Paul took a sip of coffee and then pointed outside at the end of the counter where his 1932 Ford Phaeton was parked. Kenny looked at the car, "Not that car, the big car."

"Yeah, why?"

Kenny spoke, "Can you still drive it?"

Diesel snorted and looked at Paul, "Does a fish breath underwater?"

Kenny asked, "What I mean, was it still drivable?"

Paul said, "Yeah, what are you thinking?"

"I have an idea for a backup plan."

Paul and Kenny look at each other, and then Paul and Diesel look at each other. Then Kenny put his right hand on Diesel's shoulder and said, "Hey, are you and all your old truckin' buddies still planning to meet at Owls Head this weekend?"

July 3 at 8:30 AM, Rudy's Diner, South Portland, Maine

Truck noises from the flat-screen television mounted behind the counter attracted the attention of the three men. A television news reporter reported an update on the traffic. The news screen showed Can Afford trailer trucks, Wal-Mart trailer trucks, some cars mostly connected to 'on-star' or equivalent, and rental cars all stopped in the middle of different highways, roads, and streets. Most trailer trucks that broke down on the Turnpike were in the right lane. Some were half in the right lane and the other half in the breakdown lane, with at least one reflective triangle on the road behind each trailer. Some vehicles had rear-ended trailers, cars, and trucks. Those had, in turn, been rear-ended by other stopped cars and trucks.

Old footage showed traffic moving slowly at the York, ME, toll booth. Using a landline phone, a news reporter told the in-studio reporter, "I just finished speaking with Peter Mills, the head of the Turnpike Authority. Mills said all maintenance crews were called in to assist with clearing the roadway of out-of-commission vehicles. He also said the Turnpike would keep at least two lanes open for traffic flow Northbound and Southbound. The television displayed a scene of the Turnpike's traffic status via the Turnpike Authority's cameras.

Diesel said, "Hey Paul, after looking at that, it makes guys like you and I glad we don't have to drive anymore unless we want to."

Kenny looked at his watch and said, "Hey, I got to go and relieve Truckin Bob before he kills Ron. Are you two going to be here for a while?"

Diesel answered, "Well, it sure looks like being here is a much better choice than being out there."

Kenny spoke as he started to walk towards the door, "Good, I'll try to be back before lunch."

Kenny walked out the door and got in his Ford F250 4x4. Paul told Diesel, "You know it's going to cost them a lot to make me want to drive again."

Diesel said, "That's right, we're old and slow and have a higher maintenance cost."

Paul spoke, "Gino is one of only a few mechanics that know how to work on a truck without a computer."

Diesel said, "George at Pensway he's pretty good with the older trucks. Well, at the rate it's going," Diesel pointed at the television, "the old ways of trucking with guys like you and I will have to show these young whippersnapper administrators how we made this country move."

Paul smiled, "Just like Will and Sonny."

Diesel said, "That's right."

July 3 at 8:45 AM, Can Afford dispatch.

Ron LaFlute received a return call from Del Hayes in South Carolina.

"Hello, I'm Ron LaFlute, in charge of trucking at Can Afford Warehouse in South Portland, Maine." Ron listens, "All our tractors have shut down and won't start. Our mechanics at Pensway told me that they need some security code numbers to unlock the anti-theft system."

The person at Del Hayes replied, "Sorry to inform you that information was not accessible. Our computers have shut down, and we have no idea when or even if they will turn back on."

Ron slowed his speech, "That's not what I wanted to hear. is there anybody I can talk to that has the security codes on paper files?"

The Del Hayes person replied, "No, once any information is programmed into Zaida, all paper files were shredded."

Ron spoke, "Why?"

Del Hayes representative replied, "Because paper files are no longer needed once they have been programmed into the Zaida system."

Ron said, "I think we need those paper files now! So, what are we supposed to do?" The Del Hayes sounded apologetic, "I can try to find someone else, but everyone here is in a meeting. Can Afford is not the only one with this problem. All the other grocery store chains Del Hayes owns are having similar problems. I heard Mainers are very resilient; you may have to rely on that. Meanwhile, I'll put you on hold and try to find someone else to help you."

Kenny Hews parked his pick-up in the parking lot in front of the warehouse. He looked at the digital trailer ID and placement screen near the main gate guard shack. The screen was all scribbly. Then he looked and counted all the OTR tractors at the meat dock. Kenny Hews walked up the stairs to the Can Afford dispatch office. Ron LaFlute was sitting at the dispatch desk with the phone to his ear. Ron looked at the door opening, and in walked Kenny.

Ron said, “Oh, thank God you’re here.”

Kenny said, “Yeah, I need to talk to Bob. Where is he?”

Ron said, “Do you know what has happened?”

Kenny repeated, “WHERE’S BOB?”

Ron replied, “He’s in Karen’s office.”

Kenny walked to Karen’s office. Just as he entered her office, Karen and Bob were discussing the location of the disabled tractors. They both looked up and said, “Thank God you’re here.”

Kenny said, “Isn’t that funny when the sky started falling? Everyone becomes religious.”

Bob said, “Karen’s working on locating and removing ALL the Can Afford tractors stuck in intersections first. Then the ones on the road, and finally the ones at the stores.”

Kenny spoke, “What’s the plan to get the trailers back here?”

Bob said, “We haven’t gotten that far yet. Ron has been on the phone with Del Hayes to get the tractors’ security codes.”

Bob and Kenny left Karen’s office and walked toward Ron LaFlute. Bob said, “Ron, have you got them?”

Ron said, “Del Hayes’s computers have all shut down. The person I spoke with said they don’t know when or even if they will come back up. She did say the other grocery store chains that Del Hayes owns are in the same boat we’re in.”

Bob put his right hand on his forehead and pushed his hair up while looking at Kenny. Kenny looked back at Bob and said, “Ron, did you ask about any backup files?”

Ron said, "Yes. She said the information we need was shredded once it was programmed into the Zaida system."

Kenny spoke, "So basically, we're on our own."

Ron spoke, "Yup," nodding his head.

Bob asked, "Why are you still on the phone?"

Ron said, "She put me back on hold after telling me she would try to find someone to help us."

Exasperated, Bob said, "Hang up the phone."

Ron said, "Yeah, but what if she finds somebody?"

Bob raised his voice, "Hang up the damn phone! We can't run trucking on maybes and ifs!"

Ron double-checked to hear anyone on the phone, then disconnected the call. Bob and Kenny looked at each other as Kenny turned to walk back to Karen's office. Kenny shook his head.

Bob said, "Ron, get Dave from Load-Con over here. Kenny, call Danny on the radio. I need to talk with him."

Bob walked back to Karen's office. As Bob entered her office, he said, "How are you making it?"

Karen replied, "I got the location of fifteen trucks. Four of them are blocking traffic. Seven are on the road, and three are at the docks of three stores in Mass. One was blocking the rear driveway of the New Bedford, New Hampshire store. That driver had a backhaul of Monadnock water."

"Great Job. Can you call Larry at Pensway and tell him the locations of the four trucks blocking traffic. Then tell him I'll call him in a little while about the others."

Bob walked to his desk behind dispatch, picked up the phone, and called O'Hegerty. Donald answered the phone "O'Hegerty Trucking."

Bob spoke, "Donald, It's me, Truckin Bob; I need you, Bob Tyghman, and Mark over here at dispatch in thirty minutes. Can you do me a favor? Call Wayne and Mark at Pensway and tell them I need them both over here at dispatch at the same time."

Donald said, "I won't be able to make it over there."

Bob said, "No, I need you here for your dispatching input."

Donald replied, "Ok, I'll get Joyce to hold down the fort."

The door from the stairs opened, and Danny, the yard jockey, walked in, all the while fidgeting. Kenny walked out of the driver's room with a cup of coffee.

Kenny said, "Danny, Bob needs to talk to you."

Danny said, "Where are all the company drivers? None of the Can Afford drivers have come back yet. Only five O'Hegerty drivers have come back."

Kenny replied, "I think that's part of what Bob wants to talk to you about." Bob looked over the cubicle wall at Kenny and Danny talking. Bob spoke to Donald on the phone, "I gotta go. Don't forget to call Wayne."

Bob hung up the phone and then walked over to Danny and Kenny. Bob said, "Danny, I need an inventory of every available trailer. Both dry vans and reefers, even the emergency use trailers."

Danny nodded his head. Ron and Dave from Loadcon walked around the corner by Karen's office and continued to walk toward Bob, Kenny, and Danny.

Bob turned his head to look at Ron and Dave. Then Bob looked back at Danny. Bob said, "Can you get me the list of trailers in fifteen minutes?"

Danny turned slightly to face the door, "I'll do my best."

As Danny quickly walked through the door to the stairs, Bob spoke as he looked at Dave, "Dave, how many grocery loads do we have going out today?"

Dave replied, "Eighty-seven."

Bob said, "Can you get me the list categorized with load numbers, store numbers, town, and state, and the dispatched times?"

"Yeah, it's going to take me some time."

Bob said, "Well, I need the list in about half an hour from now."

"What?" With bulging eyes and mouth open, Dave looked at Kenny.

Kenny nodded his head with a smile; Kenny said, "You can do it, Disco."

Dave turned to walk back to the Load-Con office.

Bob said, "Kenny, help Dave with that list."

Dave and Kenny walked away, with Ron following them.

Bob said, "Ron, go open up the conference room and make sure the easel board was clean with markers that work."

With a grumble, Ron turned around and walked to the conference room. Bob walked back to Karen's office.

Karen was talking to Larry at Pensway. "Bob just walked into my office. Larry needs to talk to you." Karen handed the phone to Bob.

"Larry, was Cash Corner cleared?" Bob asked.

"Yes, the tractor and trailer are being unhooked out front of the shop right now. Were you able to get the security codes?"

Bob said, "No, all Del Hayes' tractors have stopped. More or less, they said we are on our own."

"What are you going to do?"

Bob replied, "We are having a big meeting over here with your bosses and O'Hegerty in less than a half hour from now. I need you to get the Can Afford tractors disconnected from the trailers and use your tractors to bring the trailers back here to the warehouse."

Larry said, "What do you want to do with Can Afford tractors?"

Bob replied, "When you're done disconnecting from all the trailers, have the wrecker drivers drop the tractors in the vacant lot behind the freezer." Larry said, "Ok." Bob said, "I got to get ready for this meeting. Here's Karen with the rest of the locations of the tractors." Bob handed the phone to Karen.

July 3 at 8:30 AM, I-95 in New Hampshire

Albert was driving North on I-95 in New Hampshire. The speed limit has been slowed to 50 mph because of the many stopped cars, Wal*Mart trailer trucks, FedEx trucks, Can Afford trailer trucks, and Schneider trailer trucks. The only trucks moving are fuel tankers, Poland Spring tankers, Dry Van freight haulers, Sunbury Canadian Trucking—NEMF, Land Air, Old Dominion, Con-Way, Roadway, Overnite Express, and others. Some independent over-the-road drivers, Ross Express of New England trailer with a decal "Truckers keep America Rolling," Grocery Basket, a couple of Concord Trailway buses, and K & B hauling a tri-axle trailer load of compressed garbage, which really does stink on warm days.

The highway has four lanes North and four lanes South. Only two lanes were open. North traffic was flowing, zigzagging around disabled vehicles. There are a lot of people out of their cars on the right walking back and forth; some have pet dogs on leashes. A car was headed North, and the driver and the passenger were arguing over a GPS system that wasn't working.

The driver grabbed the GPS device from the passenger. The driver, not paying attention, rear-ended a Ryder Wheeler Box Truck that had broken down in the middle right lane. Some people from a broken-down Enterprise car walked from the right side of the highway to help. Two cars and a building contractor in a one-ton truck were ahead of Albert. All three vehicles pulled over to help. Albert drove by slowly and said to himself, "Damn, that's got to hurt." He looked briefly but kept driving. As Albert continued, he scanned the southbound lanes, and there sat an O'Hegerty driver with a disabled new automatic transmission tractor. Albert raised his left hand to wave.

Traffic continued to zigzag through the maze of broken-down vehicles. The brake lights started lighting up, and there was a brief shot of blue lights through the traffic, a New Hampshire State Trooper. When Albert reached the State Trooper's car, he groaned, "Damn," and quickly rolled up the driver's door window.

He saw a tri-axle trailer trash hauler rolled over on its left side in the median that divides the North and Southbound lanes. A camper trailer was smashed, and the small pick-up pulling it was smashed into a Wal*Mart trailer. Traffic flow was moving to the right lane and breakdown lane. Looking ahead after the accident, he could see the Piscataqua River Bridge that would take him into Maine.

Albert said, “Finally, I can leave this stinking state.” Traffic continued to zigzag through broken-down cars and trucks. Now, on the approach to the bridge, there are three lanes of travel northbound cut down to one lane; the speed limit has been reduced to 20 mph. In the southbound lanes, there were two lanes open for travel.

“I hope it stays that way.”

CHAPTER 6

July 3 at 8:45 AM, Can Afford Warehouse, Maine

Now back to Truckin Bob and the big meeting.

Kenny and Disco Dave were finishing the list of grocery loads and store locations.

Kenny spoke, "Disco, make five copies. While you're doing that, I will talk to Bob and check on Danny." Kenny walked around to Bob's cubicle. Kenny hesitated to speak because Bob was writing something down.

Bob said, "How are you guys making it?" Kenny spoke, "I just told Disco to make copies. O'Hegerty and Pensway will not even come close to delivering all those loads, but I do have an idea that could get us through this."

Bob prompts, "What's that?"

Kenny said, "I stopped at Rudy's this morning and spoke to Paul Garish and Diesel. They have their own tractors, and there's going to be an antique truck show at Owl's Head this weekend. Paul and Diesel are friends with all those retired truckers."

Bob's facial expression changes with a look of interest. Bob said, "Do you think they can do it?"

Kenny spoke, "They're retired, not dead. Besides, it would give them a chance to show off." Danny opened the door from the stairs and quickly walked over to Bob's desk. Danny was a little out of breath. Then he spoke, "Here you go, Bob. That's all the trailers we have."

Bob said, "Wow, that was fast, thank you, Danny."

Danny said, "Let me know if you need anything else."

Bob replied, "I will, and thanks again."

Danny walked away and into the Drivers' Lounge. Disco walked over to Bob's desk and handed the copies of all the loads. Bob said, "I knew you could do it. I have faith in you."

Disco replied, "I couldn't have done it without Kenny." Kenny just smiled and turned to look at the door from the stairs as it opened. Donald, Bob Tyghman, and Mark O'Hegerty walked in, followed by Wayne Tareault and his boss. Just then, Ron walked around the corner from the conference room. As if to take charge, he waves his hand for everybody to follow his lead to the conference room. Bob looked at Kenny, then says, "I am going to kill him."

Kenny spoke, "I know."

Bob urged, "I need you in this meeting, but we need trucks with drivers. Can you go back to Rudy's and get as many of those retirees as you can? Tell them to fuel up at the Can Afford pumps at Pensway, and we will pay them very well."

Kenny nodded his head, "We are still going to need more drivers. There are a lot of over-the-road drivers still unloading. We may be able to use them too."

Bob said, "Good idea. On your way out, can you stop at Receiving and tell them not to let any of the drivers leave? I'll go to Receiving after this meeting."

Kenny nodded again, "I'll be back with the cavalry. Don't

kill Ron until I get back. I don't want to miss the white flag."

Bob with a smirk grabbed all the papers off his desk. Bob and Kenny looked at each other, and Bob said, "I'll try. That's all I'm saying."

Kenny leaves, going through the door to the stairwell. Bob walked to the conference room. As he approaches the room, he can hear Ron boasting and talking about his authority and direction and that Truckin Bob and Kenny Hewey are following his orders. Then, with his professional trucking dispatch experience, "We all work together as a team, and we will get through this dilemma."

As Truckin Bob walked through the door to the conference room, Ron's expression changed to an 'oh shit, I'm in trouble' look. Ron quickly raised his right hand, motioning for Bob to come over.

Ron said, "Oh good, Bob, you're here, come up and explain our dilemma."

Bob approached the easel and said, "As you know, all Can Afford tractors are dead."

"No, they...." Ron tried to correct Bob.

Bob continued raising his voice above Ron's, "They're dead right now." Ron was silent.

"Mark, I know some of your tractors are dead, also. Are you having any luck with getting them started?" Bob asked.

Mark replied, "Well, Wayne has been trying to call the security software company that monitors those tractors. He hasn't been able to get through."

Mark and Wayne look at each other. Wayne said, "Mark's tractors are in the same status as Can Afford tractors."

"Alright, we'll need every available tractor from O'Hegerty and Pensway. Now, Mark, we will need every trailer you have," Bob directed, and Mark nodded.

Bob continued, "Wayne, can you coordinate with the tow trucks to bring a non-dead tractor with them? That way, the Can Afford driver can bring back the Can Afford trailer."

"Yes, I was going to suggest that."

Bob said, "Good. We will have to use some of the Yard Use Only trailers. Wayne, can you get your trailer shop and Great Dane Trailer Shop to check out these trailers?" Bob handed Wayne a copy of the trailer list created by Danny.

Wayne asked, "What kind of repairs do you want to be done if needed?"

Bob said, "Tires, brakes, lights, fuel tanks, and refrigeration, nothing cosmetic."

Wayne said, "OK."

Bob turned to the easel, grabbed a marker, and wrote the number of grocery loads on the board, then drew three columns, one for each state, Maine, New Hampshire, and Massachusetts.

Bob turned to the dispatch operators, "Now Donald, you and Kenny will have to work the loads as time tight as you can get them. Emphasize to your drivers that they must return here as soon as possible."

"Where's Kenny?" asked Donald.

"He's out recruiting some drivers with their own tractors as we speak."

"What?" Ron almost shouted.

Bob calmly replied as he looked at Ron, "We don't have enough drivers, tractors, and trailers to get all these loads out." Bob pointed to the easel.

"Who's he getting?" Ron asked, nearly spitting.

Bob said, "I don't know; all he said was he'll be back with the calvary."

Donald said, "Bob, do you have a list of the grocery loads?"

Bob spoke as he sorted through papers and handed the Can Afford Dead Tractor list and locations to Wayne, "Wayne, here's the list and locations of all the dead Can Afford tractors." Bob looked at Ron expecting him to say something.

Bob handed the grocery loads list to Donald. Bob continued, "Wayne, I talked to Larry earlier. I want the tractors blocking traffic moved first. Those are the red-highlighted ones. Larry knows the rest."

Donald spoke, "When was Kenny coming back?"

Bob said, "Soon, I hope."

Ron interrupted, "I want to know who these drivers are that Kenny was bringing here. They're not pulling any Can Afford trailers till I approve."

Bob looked at Donald. Bob pursed his mouth, rolled his eyes, and clenched the papers. "Until then, Ron, can you go to Grocery and the freezer to find out if they'll have enough staff?"

Ron said, "Good idea. If they are short of help, I'll get the PRC staff to help."

Bob said, "Great idea, Ron. I don't know how Grocery could do it without your guidance and experience."

Ron said, "That's right."

Bob spoke as he pointed to the clock on the wall, "You better hurry up before we get any further behind schedule."

Ron said, "Right, right, page me when Kenny gets back here." Ron quickly walked out of the conference room.

"Kenny asked me not to kill him until he was here to watch," Bob said through gritted teeth.

Donald laughed, "Have Kenny call me when he gets back."

Bob said, "I will." Then Donald left the conference room. Bob walked to the phone on the wall and called Grocery Receiving.

Jeff spoke, "Jeff, Grocery Receiving."

Bob said, "Truckin' Bob here; I just sent Ron to help you."

"I don't need his help."

Bob said, "I know you don't. I need a big favor from you. Can you find Ron something to do for a few hours?"

"What!" Jeff huffed.

"I know, I know, I'll have a lobster cook-out and plenty of Sam Adams beer after we get through all this crap," Bob promised.

Jeff said, "Boston Lager."

"Ok, just remind me later."

Jeff said, "Oh, speak of the devil; Ron just got here, got to go."

Bob said, "Hey, thanks a lot. Talk to you later."

July 3 at 9:15 AM, Rudy's Diner, South Portland, ME

Kenny spoke, "Bob and I know this will be a lot to ask you two and your trucker buddies. We know you guys won't be able to do it all, so I stopped at Meat and Produce Receiving before coming here and talked to the over-the-road drivers."

Diesel said, "What did they say?" Paul and Diesel look at each other and then back to Kenny.

"Well, a few hemmed and hawed, and a couple said no, but

after I said they would get free fuel plus mileage pay, they all said yes." Both Paul and Diesel grinned and nodded.

Kenny said, "Now, with you two and all your buddies, how many tractors are we looking at?" Paul and Diesel quoted some names. Paul made some marks on a paper napkin with his pen.

After Paul counted, he said, "Twenty-five to thirty tractors."

"Great! I'll try to give them all the Maine trips, maybe a few New Hampshire trips, to you guys. The Mass and the long New Hampshire trips to the over-the-road drivers. Where and when are you all going to meet?"

Diesel spoke, "Well, last time I talked to John, we were all going to meet at the Maine Mall around 10:30 and have lunch at Sebago Brewing Company."

"Great, stick to that plan. I'll try to get as many Maine loads as possible and be ready a little after noon. Oh, do you think some of you guys might be able to do some morning loads for tomorrow?"

Paul and Diesel looked at each other. Paul said, "I might be able to as long as I get some sleep after the grocery load."

Diesel said, "That goes for me too, but I can't say that for the other guys." Paul and Diesel looked and nodded at each other.

Kenny said, "You tell them, and this includes you two, Can Afford will put you up at HoJo's down the street."

Diesel said, "Some of those guys would like that." Paul nodded again.

Kenny added, "Make sure they all know to fuel up at Pensway at the Can Afford fuel pump and I'll have directions for everybody. I got to go; I'll see you after lunch, and again, thanks a lot."

Kenny walked outside to his pick-up truck. Diesel sat on the stool beside Paul, put one elbow on the counter, and leaned back on the counter facing the street as he watched Kenny leave. Kenny held out his left hand to stop a South Portland Police car and spoke briefly with the officer. The officer gave Kenny a nod and a thumbs up.

Diesel said, "I can't wait to see the look on Ron's face when we old farts show up."

With a slight grin, Paul said, "Isn't it funny how his new technically advanced fleet of trucks was supposed to be faster and stronger. Look who's bailing his stupid, arrogant ass out. Us, too old and too slow truck drivers."

"Yeah, the sun gets indigestion and stops all those new trucks. Hell, when we would eat a bowl of Rudy's chili, that didn't even slow us down. We'd grab some Rolaids and Tums and keep going."

Paul nodded his head, "Yup."

July 3 at 9:50 AM, I-95 after the Scarborough Exit

Albert looked to the right, after the Scarborough exit, and saw a lot of black Kenworth tractors parked at R C Moore Trucking, and a group of men were walking out of the office and toward the Kenworths. Then he saw traffic slow down at the Maine Mall exit. As he approached the toll booth, he saw a WGME Channel 13 TV News van and camera crew. The WGME crew watched Albert drive by.

July 3 at 9:55 AM, Ruby's Diner, South Portland, Maine

Back at Rudy's, Paul and Diesel were looking at the television, and Diesel spoke, "Hey, isn't that Albert?"

"Yeah, it is. If there was any one of O'Hegerty's drivers to make it back from Boston through all that crap, it would be him," Paul said with a chuckle.

The television report continued, "That's a good sign for Can Afford. Can Afford Supermarkets has O'Hegerty Trucking pulling their trailer."

"What will that reporter say when we start pulling Can Afford trailers? Should we stop and tell them?" Diesel asked.

"No, I don't need the publicity. I'm only doing it because Kenny asked."

"Yeah, you're right. I wouldn't do it either if it wasn't for Kenny. You must admit it will be worth it just to see Ron's face," Diesel laughed.

"Yup."

July 3 at 10:00 AM, Can Afford Warehouse, So.Portland, Maine

Albert drove through Can Afford Warehouses' Main Entrance Gate. He stopped at the gatehouse and reported to security, "Produce Market load." He handed the State Garden shipping papers to the security person in the gatehouse.

The security person called Produce Receiving. "Hey, State Garden load. What door do you want it in?" The security person marked the State Garden paperwork "Door 44" and circled it. After he hung up the phone, he returned the paperwork to Albert and directed, "44 Door."

"Thanks; hey, do you know of any empty O'Hegerty trailers over here?" Albert asked.

"Yeah, there's a couple across from the freezer dock."

"I have to go back to the Produce Market for a second load," Albert said.

The security person looked at Albert and replied, "Good luck with that; you'll need it."

Albert replied, "I know. Thanks again." Albert drove to the Produce dock, backed into dock door 44, and disconnected from the Can Afford trailer. Then he drove to the freezer and hooked up to an O'Hegerty trailer.

Albert drove through the main gate and waved at the security person in the gatehouse. The security person waved back. Albert went into Pensway's yard and up to the fuel island. Steve filled up the tractor "145" and the trailer.

Steve asked, "Are you returning to the Produce Market?"

Albert replied, "Yup, and it will suck trying to get back." Steve responded by nodding his head, then asked, "Oh, yeah, it is. How's your wife doing?"

"Tired. She's hanging in there."

"Has Felicia made it back from Oregon yet?"

Albert replied, "Yes, she made it back yesterday. Her friend, Kayla, came with her."

Steve said, "That's good. The national news on the radio just said all airline flights have been canceled until we get through this solar crap."

Albert said, "Great, 95 sucks for driving; it's going to suck even more."

Steve said, "Yeah, but you got a Kenworth; you can push any dumb ass that gets in your way."

Albert replied, "True, but I don't want to scratch the bumper."

Steve finished fueling up the trailer. He said, "There, I'll see you when you get back. Just remember, don't let anybody slow you down."

"Thanks. Can you do me a favor? Just in case I don't get back by 2:30?"

Then Steve replied, "Sure, what?"

Albert spoke, "Felicia, Kayla, and Marc are going to Maine Med to see Michelle. Can you make sure they get there?"

"Yeah, I may be called in early to work at the fire department. What room is Michelle in?" asked Steve.

"Room 309, Cardiac ICU next to the OR. Jenny the waitress at Rudy's knows where the room is." Albert opened the tractor door, got in the cab, closed the door, and started the engine.

"Thanks, again, I'll see you later." said Albert as he drove out of the fuel island to go back to the Produce Market.

July 3 at 9:20 AM, Cash Corner Intersection

After Kenny stopped the police officer at the intersection, he talked with him. The officer nodded his head as Kenny drove away.

CHAPTER 7

July 3 at 9:00 AM, Arecibo Observatory, Puerto Rico

At the Arecibo Observatory in Puerto Rico, the scientists that were watching the sun. Computer screens were showing some larger flare-ups. One scientist said, "Should I call NASA?"

The second scientist said, "Yes, hopefully, Carmelo, they know already."

Carmelo called NASA.

NASA operator answered, "NASA, John F. Kennedy Space Center, how may I direct your call?"

"I need to speak to Clint Wood, extension 309."

The operator responds, "One moment, please," then transfers the call.

"Clint Wood, Solar Dynamics Observatory," Clint Wood answered not really listening to the other end of the conversation.

"This was Carmelo Burgos at Arecibo, are you seeing what we're seeing?"

NASA scientist answered, "Thank you for calling, yes. Have you calculated the intensity of this solar flare?"

Carmelo answered, "Norman Vicenty was doing that as we speak. With these Coronal Mass Ejections, there are going to be massive power grid blackouts. Norman has been calculating where and when."

NASA scientist Clint cautioned, "The lobby is filling up with news reporters. They are asking how long these solar flares are going to last."

Norman excitedly answered, "I've got it. My best guess, based on Butterfly Diagram Variables, the northeast of the United States, the brunt should be in the Atlantic Ocean."

NASA scientist said, "New England only?"

"No, New York and the upper half of New Jersey."

Clint questioned, "Any guesses of the cause for these flares and how many more of these CME waves are coming?"

"Yes, an asteroid field has come close to the sun. The larger asteroid pieces must be composed of iron, methane, nitrogen, and oxygen to create the flare ups. The smaller pieces burn up before they reach the surface of the sun. To answer, how long will this solar storm last? It's hard to tell. We can't see the end of the asteroid field yet," Norman said.

At NASA another call came in on the same phone. It started to ring, and the screen displayed an extension number and name. NASA scientist Clint interjected, "I've got to go, Bill Jones, NASA's Press Rep was on the other line. Again, thank you for this update and let us know when you see the end of the asteroid field."

Norman replied, "Yes, I will. Good-bye."

July 3 at 10:05 AM, Can Afford Warehouse, Scarborough, Maine

Kenny drove into the O'Hegerty trucking driveway, parked, and walked into its dispatch office. Seeing Donald he asked,

"How are you making it?"

Donald said, "I've got five automatic day cabs that won't move and three sleeper automatics that won't move either. But we do have twenty standard tractors, ten, maybe twelve, will be ready to go by noon."

"Great. Just for the heads up, I just came from Rudy's. I talked with Paul Garish and Diesel. A little after noon, they are bringing twenty-five to thirty of their buddies with antique tractors through the warehouse gate."

"Wow," breathed Donald, with eyes wide open and a wide smile.

Kenny continued, "I told them I would give them all the Maine trips and a few New Hampshire trips."

"That's fine. I mean, great, that will be impressive to see. What's Ron going to say?" Donald asked.

"He can't say anything because Bob will duct tape a pole with a white flag to his arm and tie him to the Main Gate." Donald and Kenny laugh.

"Bob would do that. Tell Bob I'll hold Ron's arm!" joked Donald.

"You'll have to stand in line for that one," Kenny looked at the clock and continued speaking, "I'm sure Bob must be fit to be tied himself. I got to go. I'll give you a call on the loads shortly."

July 3 at 10:40 AM, Southbound lane of I-95, New Hampshire

Albert was driving south through New Hampshire. Two lanes were open for travel, approximately 55 mph, but northbound traffic was very slow, two lanes open, approximately 30 to 35 mph.

Albert looked at the miles of traffic going North and exclaimed, "Damn it." Then he moved into the left lane and passed an Old Neighborhood "Thin & Trim" meat truck from Lynn, MA. The tractor was an older Mack. Albert spoke on the CB to the Old Neighborhood driver, "Hey driver from the Old Neighborhood! Smile. That old dog can out pull a new Can Afford tractor even on a sunny day."

The Old Neighborhood driver replied, "You got that right!" As they both drove by a Can Afford driver parked in the right lane and the breakdown lane. Albert tooted the air horn and waved to the Can Afford driver. The Can Afford driver looked as Albert drove by and shook his head with a partly left-hand wave and a lost look on his face. Albert smiled and continued driving. He turned on the AM/FM radio to listen to 105.7, WROR for any traffic updates.

Music was playing. The song ended and Loran announced, "Wally, I think we need to hear an extra 'Men from Maine.' Kinda fitting as it was the story of Ephus driving the wrong way on the Maine Turnpike."

"Loran, here's a song fitting also, 'The Bridge in Borne.'"

After the song was over Hank Morse has an update on the traffic. "The Massachusetts and New Hampshire State Police are urging people to not travel. All the major highways and roads are filled with cars and trucks that can't move because of electrical problems caused by the solar flares. They also said anybody using a GPS for directions, forget it, none of them work."

Wally asked, "What will the people use to go on vacation?"

Loran said, "What do you mean? Have you ever heard of a map? That's what I use, it's always worked for me!"

"Yeah, but not everybody knows how to use a map."

"If you can't read a map, you should never go on a road trip!" Loran quipped.

Albert nodded his head as he looked at his driver's bag filled with map books.

Wally spoke on the air, "Oh my God, bad news. NASA was reporting we are going to lose power very soon."

"What are you talking about, Wally?"

"NASA called a press conference with reporters in Florida. A NASA representative said there was another solar flare happening right now and it's going to shut down the power grid in the northeastern area of the United States."

"Did he say when we're going to lose power?" Loran asked.

"Yes, between twenty to thirty minutes from now!"

Albert heard the news, "Shit." Then he downshifted, accelerated, and started passing cars and trucks, zigzagging through traffic.

Albert noticed two Can Afford trucks and their drivers in the northbound lanes of Rt. 95. The same two Can Afford drivers that commented on Albert's Kenworth tractor saying that it was junk, were now standing beside one of the disabled Can Afford tractors. One of the drivers started to say, "You know..." The other driver said, "Don't even say it."

Albert was driving south, passing everything going slow, sometimes moving his rig onto the grass in the median. He finally made it to Route One in Peabody, MA. Just as Albert approached the one traffic light, the power grid shut down and the green light went dark. Albert looked at the AM/FM radio and tried to turn the volume up. No music was playing. "Damn it." He reached down with his left hand and flipped on the clutch fan switch, then the engine sound grew louder, and Albert pulled over to the far-left lane and stepped on the accelerator.

As Albert approached the Lynn exit, looking up and over to the left, cars were stopped because the traffic lights were not working. The car drivers were yelling and honking their horns at each other. Albert stayed in the far-left lane, making it to the off ramp to Logan Airport at the town line of Saugus and Revere. The traffic was backed up south and north on Route 1.

"Shit." He continued past the off ramp and traffic started moving again. He looked at Route One—northbound traffic was all stopped. "I'm not going that way back to Maine." He drove to the Carter Street exit, made a left at the Hess gas station and crossed over the railroad tracks. The traffic stopped.

Albert looked ahead to the traffic light at Mass General and saw a three-car accident. Immediately, Albert turned right into the Grocery Basket parking lot, drove through the lot and came out by State Garden, then took a side street into the produce market.

Gonzo was exiting through the gate to the BMT at the same time Albert was entering. They both stop, Albert asked, "What do you need me to do?"

Gonzo quickly gave Albert instructions, "Go to Tavilla's, pick up eighteen pallets, refrigerate at forty degrees then go to Matarazzo's Plant for six pallets of tomatoes. That's your load."

Albert said, "Hey, thanks. Don't go Route One North, every lane was stopped."

"Great, I got beer on ice waiting at home. By the time I get home the ice will be melted, and the beer will be warm. This shit really sucks," Gonzo complained.

Albert said, "Yeah, it does. We need to get going, the longer we're here the worse it's going to get."

"You're right. See ya." Gonzo drove away toward the BMT Building and Albert drove in the opposite direction toward Tavilla's.

July 3 at 10:00 AM, Rudy's Diner, South Portland

Now back to Maine to the antique trucks. Paul stood up from the stool, reached onto the counter and grabbed his car keys, "Well, I gotta go trade cars and clean the cobwebs off the steering wheel. I'll meet you at Sebago's Brewing Restaurant."

While Paul and Diesel were talking, an older black Lincoln Continental parked in front of the diner. An older man exited the car and walked through the front door. Paul's back was to the door.

Diesel sat at the counter looking past Paul to the door as the older man walked into the restaurant. Diesel smiled and said, "Look who's walking in, Father Time of trucking!"

Paul turned toward to the door, "Hey Joe, it's been a while, how have you been?" As Paul and Joe shook hands, Diesel got up and shook Joe's hand.

"Joe, I bet you're glad your son, Mark, is running O'Hegerty Trucking, especially now with this solar crap going on," said Diesel.

Joe asked, "What the hell's wrong with all the Can Afford trucks?"

"You haven't heard?"

Joe said, "Heard what?"

Paul explained, "The sun has had some large solar flare ups which have wiped out several satellites in space. Ironically, Can Afford's entire computerized tractor fleet was controlled by one of those satellites. Now all their tractors are dead."

Joe shook his head, "I warned Mark about that when he bought those automatic transmission tractors. That's why I'm still driving that old Lincoln because it doesn't need a computer."

"I'd love to stay and talk with you, Joe, but Diesel and I promised Kenny Hewey we would pull some grocery loads for him. So, I've got to go home and trade cars."

Joe said, "Paul, leave your car here, I'll give you a ride home."

The waitress, Jenny, stood at the counter next to Paul, Joe, and Diesel. "Leave your keys here in case I need to move it."

Paul placed the keys on the counter in front of Jenny and said, "No drag racing." The waitress made a face, "Yeah, right."

Diesel laughed. Paul stepped toward the door, "Ok Joe, let's go." Paul and Joe leave together, getting into the Lincoln Continental, and drive to Paul's house on a farm in Westbrook, Maine.

As they drive to Paul's house, Joe continued to complain about computers. "I'd like to meet the dumbass engineer that thought a computer could drive a truck better than we could. I would punch him square in the face. Then, when he looked up at me with his face in his hand with a why did you do that look, I'd say, 'what, your iPhone's intuition or gut feeling didn't tell you that was coming.' Dumbass."

Paul and Joe laugh.

"You're right, Joe, a computer has its uses but not in a truck-driving ability." He lowered his voice and continued, "It just turned truck drivers into lazy steerers."

"Exactly." Joe and Paul reached Paul's driveway and Joe spoke continued, "Where do you keep the old Clydesdale?"

"Just inside the door on the right." Joe parked the Lincoln in front of the left door of a huge red barn, turned the engine off, and they both got out. Paul walked over to the left door and opened it. Joe walked around the back of the Lincoln and looked at Paul grabbing a rope on the right. The rope led straight up to a pulley wheel which went to another pulley wheel in the center. The rope then came forward to another hanging pulley wheel at the center, connected to a pad eye center of a 2" x 4" x 14' which has a big sheet blanket connected to it. Paul pulled downward on the rope, then it stopped. The two by four and blanket rose as Paul pulled the rope. While holding the rope with his left hand, Paul used his right hand to untie another rope, then he let it go. He continued pulling the first rope down and the two by four with the blanket lifted uncovering a large steel bumper and a chrome radiator grill. At the top front of the grill was the name 'Autocar' in chrome. Joe walked over to Paul as he finished pulling the blanket off the dual chrome exhaust stacks. Paul tied the rope to the anchor on a wall beam.

Joe said, "Does that sheet keep it warm during the winter?"

"No, but it does keep the barn swallows from shitting all over it."

Joe looked up at the rope, pulleys, and blanket, "That's quite innovative."

"Yeah, Albert came up with the idea."

Joe asked, "Really? You know Adam Smith said that Albert's his 911 driver." Paul smiled and Joe continued, "I asked Adam why. He said when everyone else fails, Albert will get the job done, no matter what."

"Joe, I trained Albert. At the end of his first week, he was on his own, unlike some of the drivers that go out with Jerry."

Joe nodded, "I know, I have to remind myself sometimes Mark has to run the company now, not me."

"Yeah, but I think you keep Mark on his toes when you show up unexpectedly and start talking with Donald or Adam before you talk with him," Paul chuckled.

"Speaking of the office, Paul, I should stop by to see if he needs any help," Joe said.

"With this solar flare problem, I think old school experience is going to be," Paul raised his voice, "in high demand for a while. I need to get over to Sebago Brewing Company Restaurant to meet up with Diesel and all the other retired drivers."

Joe started to walk back to the Lincoln, then stopped and turned back to speak to Paul, "Paul, are you all set? Do you need me to do anything?"

"No, I'm all set. Thanks for the ride home." Joe nodded. Paul continued, "Could you check on Jenny when she gets out of work at the diner? She wants to go to Maine Med and visit with Michelle, Albert's wife."

"Sure, when does she get done at the diner?"

Paul answered, "I think it's 3 o'clock." Paul opened the driver's door of the forest green colored Autocar and sat in the driver's seat. Paul's right hand grabbed the shifting lever and moved it back and forth to make sure it was in neutral, put his left foot on the clutch pedal, turned on the starter key then pressed the starter button.

Joe stood beside the Lincoln driver's door to watch Paul as he drove the Autocar out of the barn. Joe watched, with a smile and a thumbs up. Paul pulled the parking brake then got out of the Autocar to close the barn doors. Then he returned to the driver's seat of the Autocar and pushed the parking brake.

In the meantime, Joe has turned the Lincoln around. Now Joe waved at Paul as Paul waved back. Joe led the way out of Paul's driveway. Paul followed as black smoke came out of both chrome exhaust pipes. Next door, one of Paul's neighbors, mowing his lawn, waved and Paul waved back. Joe and Paul stopped at the traffic light on Payne Road, the light turned green as Joe turned left. Paul followed, but just as he drove into the intersection all the traffic lights turned off. Paul looked ahead and saw all the other traffic lights go dark.

Paul yelled, "What the hell?"

Joe kept driving then turned right to go on the spur that takes you back to O'Hegerty' office. Paul turned right into Sebago Brewing Company restaurant, then drove up alongside Diesel's cabover Kenworth. Paul pulled the parking brake, left the engine running, got out of the truck, and started to walk toward the restaurant. Just then Diesel and the other retired drivers were walking out.

Paul said, "All the traffic lights just turned off."

"Yeah, the restaurant just lost power also," Diesel said.

"Hell, we haven't gone anywhere yet and it's already getting worse."

Diesel said, "We can handle it. Hey, I've told everybody

about us doing Hewey a favor. They all said they would help. A few hemmed and hawed. Any questions, hold them for Hewey."

"You still got the power booster hooked up to your CB?" asked Paul.

"Yeah, you?"

Paul answered, "Yup, good, with the way things are going, we will need to communicate. We should tell everybody about fueling up, time and mileage."

Diesel and Paul, with the other retired truckers, were leaving the Sebago Brewing Restaurant. Paul and Diesel speaking at the same time, "Remember to keep track of your mileage and your time at each store and fill up with fuel at Pensway—your trucks and the Can Afford trailers.

Paul put his hand on Diesel's right shoulder, "You should lead the parade."

Diesel disagreed, "No, you should! Just in case some dead cars block our way there, you can push them out of the way with that bumper of yours!" Paul looked at Diesel, Paul had a half grin on his face. Diesel continued speaking, "By the time we get done with this adventure your truck will have a bumper of many colors. Maybe Dolly Parton will sing a song about it." They both laughed as they got into their trucks.

Paul revved the engine and some black exhaust puffed out of the dual exhaust pipes. Then he turned on the CB to Channel 19, grabbed his mic and said, "Everyone ready?" The other drivers started pulling their air horns, Paul started driving with Diesel and all the other truckers following. The news reporter with the camera man at the toll booth heard the air horns.

"What was that?" exclaimed the camera man.

The news reporter looked through the trees to an on ramp and saw the trucks. The news reporter pointed, "Get your camera to focus over there." The camera man with a smile on his face, "Wow! Talk about going back in time."

The cameraman focused on the tractors as they approached onto the spur and headed toward Route One.

As Paul drove approaching the traffic light on Rt. 1, a South Portland police officer stopped traffic on Rt. 1 and waved Paul and all the other drivers through. Paul and Diesel drove by Rudy's Diner tooting their air horns. The waitress was outside waving to them. As Paul made a right-hand turn into the Industrial Park, he looked straight ahead at the Cash Corner intersection and saw two tow trucks moving wrecked cars from the intersection. Paul turned right into the Industrial Park and shook his head.

Diesel spoke into his CB mic, "Stupid is as stupid does."

"Kenny is going to owe us a big one if that's what the rest of our day is going to look like," Paul said.

As the parade of tractors drove toward the Can Afford Warehouse Gate, they all passed the O'Hegerty Trucking office on the left. Donald, Bob, Mark, and Joe O'Hegerty were outside the office looking and discussing the tractors available.

Bob heard the tractors driving by, "Look," pointing at the tractors.

"What the..., who are they?" Mark asks.

Donald answered, "Kenney Hewey said he asked Paul Garish, Diesel, and a bunch of their friends with antique trucks to pull some trailer loads for Can Afford."

Joe pointed at Paul's truck, "Yeah, there's Paul leading the way, as he should." The antique tractors are approaching the main gate. A young security guard quickly got up out of the chair in the security shack. The older security guard grabbed the younger guard by the arm and said, "Kenny Hewey said they were coming." The older security guard opened the gate and all the tractors drove through the gate and turn left and head toward the dispatch office parking area.

CHAPTER 8

July 3 at 9:45 AM, Can Afford Warehouse

Ron was talking to Jeff at the grocery Shipping and Receiving desk. Ron showed Jeff a piece of paper with a list of trailer numbers and dock doors. Ron said, "These trailers are loaded, I'm going outside to tell Danny to start pulling them and put empty trailers in their place."

Jeff said, "Great idea." Ron strutted away with a smile on his face, then he spoke to himself, "They can't do this without me." Outside the employee parking lot Danny dropped the fifth Cat generator trailer and Maintenance hooked it up to the power transfer transformers.

Outside, across from the grocery dock door were empty parking spaces for trailers. All the antique tractors were parked in those spaces. Paul and Diesel parked the tractors at the security office parking spaces. Ron came outside from the grocery receiving strutting. He suddenly stopped with a surprised, shocked look on his face. Ron said, "What the hell's this?"

Ron looked at Paul and Diesel getting out of their tractors. Ron quickly walked over to them, "What? What the hell are you doing here?"

Paul and Diesel smiled and replied, "We heard your highly

advanced trucking fleet died. Kenny Hewey asked us to help him, not you."

"Nobody's pulling a Hannaford trailer out of this yard until I approve."

Paul said, "That's not what Hewey said."

"I don't care what Hewey said or anybody else. I'm the one in charge of trucking, not Kenny."

Diesel said, "Well, you'll have to tell dispatch you're the boss."

Ron straightened his back, pulled his shoulders back, stuck his chest out and looked down his nose at Paul and Diesel. Ron spoke, "I will." Ron quickly walked toward the door to the stairwell to dispatch.

Diesel said, "Do you think Ron will ever realize he has to look up to us and most everybody here."

Paul said, "No."

Now all the other drivers were walking from their tractor and toward Paul and Diesel. Paul and Diesel walked toward the door. Ron went in. Paul stopped, turned to the other drivers, and spoke, "Kenny, the head of dispatch said there will be directions for all the trips."

Diesel opened the door, "As Teddy Joy would say, it's time to face the music."

Paul smiled and led the way up the stairs. Just as they are getting near the top of the stairs, they can hear Ron complaining, "All these drivers are too old and physically not fit, and neither are their old junk trucks."

Paul and all the other drivers walked into dispatch. Ron's back was facing the drivers. Ron continued to rant at Kenny, "I'm the one in charge of trucking, not you or anybody else. I say they're not pulling any Can Afford loads out of here."

Truckin Bob was at the filing cabinet in a small room near dispatch pulling out two large thick notebooks full of store directions. Bob slammed the filing cabinet drawer shut and came out of the small room with the notebooks and a really pissed off look on his face. Bob placed the two store direction notebooks down rather hard on the second dispatch desk. Ron closed his mouth with a look of "shit" on his face. Bob turned to Ron and grabbed Ron's shirt by his collar. Bob growled, "Listen to me, you short dick Frenchman, you're not in charge, I am. Your arrogant incompetence put us here and we're damn lucky to have these retired drivers who are willing to help. They are all more than physically fit to pulling loads for us than you are at wiping your ass. Now either you help us or get the hell out of here."

Ron's face changed color to pale white with a really scared look. Ron's feet were barely touching the floor with his toes. Ron looked at the two notebooks on the desks. Ron pointed a shaking hand at the notebooks. Ron said, "I can help with the directions."

Bob put Ron down and started to let go of his shirt. Bob re-tightened his grip, "You fuck this up and I'll put you through that window. Do you understand?"

Ron's head nodded up and down, his bottom lip trembled as he replied, "Yes, sir." Bob released Ron's shirt. Ron asked Bob, "Can I go to the bathroom?" in a apprehensive voice.

Bob said, "Yes, don't forget to wash your hands."

Ron quickly walked through the retired drivers, "Excuse me, excuse me, coming through."

Diesel spoke, "Can I see that again?"

Kenny said, "I wished I had video recorded it."

Disco walked around the corner in front of the Dispatch Desk. Disco grinned, "I did," with an iPhone in his hand.

Everybody laughed.

Truckin Bob said, "Disco, it's good to know you're here to give us more than a Kodak moment."

"Hell, it will make an awesome YouTube video as soon as the internet comes back up." Disco jokes.

Kenny smiled along with Paul and Diesel, and Bob said, "In the meantime, Disco, I need you to help Kenny give out the paperwork for these loads."

Bob put his hand on one of three stacks of load diagrams on the counter in front of Kenny. Bob continued speaking, "And when Ron comes out from his ordeal in the bathroom you can help him get the directions matched up with the loads."

Disco's face changes to an 'oh shit do I have to' look.

Bob smiled and spoke, "Yes, there's a cost to putting my face on the internet."

Now Ron returned to the dispatch area drying his hands with a paper towel, "I'm ready."

"Perfect timing," Bob put his hand on Disco's shoulder, "now you and Mr. Square Pants can match up the directions with the loads." Bob finished with a smile.

Disco has a 'damn, this job sucks' look on his face. Kenny was sorting through the load diagrams marked N.H. for New Hampshire. He pulled one load diagram out and places it beside a New York Giants coffee cup. Then Kenny sorts through the load diagrams marked MASS for Massachusetts. He pulled one load diagram out and places it on the other side of the Giants cup.

Bob spoke to address the retired drivers, "I'd like to thank you all for helping us. Especially when you're supposed to be enjoying your retirement. All of you will be well paid. Please, if you can, keep a log of your time and miles. I know you know your way around New England like the back of your hands. There will be maps and word directions with every load. If you have any questions, don't hesitate to ask dispatch." Bob raised his right arm and pointed toward Kenny, Disco, and Ron.

Kenny nodded his head, Disco smiled, and Ron lifted his left hand up to wave.

Disco pulled Ron's hand down. Ron looked at Disco and asked, "What?"

"Just smile," Disco whispers as Ron was trying to smile.

Kenny looked to the left at Ron. Kenny raised his right eyebrow and shook his head.

Bob continued speaking, "Before you leave with your loads, fuel-up your tractors and the trailers at the Can Afford fuel pump at Pensway across the street from here. Just for your information, when we get through this failure of the advanced technology crisis, there will be a cook-out Bar-B-Que outside, here for all of you that have so generously come to Can Afford's rescue. Again, personally, I can't thank you enough." All the retired drivers and their wives replied with smiles and head nodding for this acknowledgement. Bob looked at all the retired drivers and smiled.

Bob approached Kenny, "Have you got Diesel's load?"

Kenny grabbed the load diagram paper from beside the Giants coffee cup and handed it to Bob. Bob stepped over to Diesel, handed him the papers for his load.

"When you come back from Dover, NH, can you do some yard jockeying? Danny hasn't stopped since he came in at 3:30 a.m. I'm not counting on any Can Afford drivers until they're here," said Bob.

Diesel said, "Yeah, sure. Bob, when was the last time you got some sleep?" Bob said, "I woke up around 10 o'clock yesterday morning."

"You need to get some sleep."

Bob replied, "Yeah, I will soon. Kenny's here now, he'll keep things going. Donald from O'Hegerty will be helping him."

Paul stepped beside Diesel and Bob and reached out to shake Bob's hand. "Great short speeches, especially the first one with Ron."

"Well, I have a short fuse when I haven't slept," admitted Bob.

Kenny urged, "Paul," Paul looked at Kenny, Kenny picked up the other load diagram from the Giant's coffee cup and extended his arm out to Paul.

Paul said, "Duty calls." Paul stepped over to Kenny.

Kenny spoke, "A straight Peabody drop and hook. Do you think you could continue on to Saugus and pick up some dunnage? They have been crying for two days now." Paul replied, "Yeah, sure."

Paul and Diesel stepped away from the dispatch desk counter as other retired drivers came for their paperwork. Paul said, "I'm going to fill up my cup with coffee. I got a feeling it's gonna be hell to pay to get back here."

Diesel replied, "You're probably right."

Diesel, Paul, and some of the other retired drivers start going down the stairs. Diesel said, "I'm going to Dover, NH then coming back to do some yard jockeying. I'll call you on my radio when I get back to see how you're making it."

"I will be at a snail's pace coming back." Paul said as they made it to the door and went outside.

Diesel said, "Keep it under a hundred."

Paul spoke with a smirk, "I'll try." They both climbed into their tractors. Paul, then Diesel drove their tractors to the Grocery dock doors. Paul looked at the load diagram to verify the trailer number matched the one at the dock door and it did. Both Paul and Diesel drove forward in front of the trailers they were picking up, then backed up to hook up to the trailers.

Now that Paul and Diesel were all hooked up to their trailers, they drove forward about ten feet and set the parking brake. They both got out of the tractors, walked to the back of the trailer, kicked the tires, and looked under the trailer at the axles. They closed the trailer doors, then locked the right door, checked the trailer lights, and they both walked back to their tractors. Diesel grabbed the CB mic, "Go ahead. I followed you in here and I'll follow you out."

Paul led the way out through the Main Gate. As they drove through the Warehouse Yard they waved at the other retired drivers as they were hooking up to their trailers. They all waved back. Paul and Diesel left the Warehouse Yard passing the Security Shack. They almost stopped at the stop sign then Paul stomped on it and the engine roared. Paul and Diesel came to the entrance to Pensway's yard, and they both drove into the yard. As they went by O'Hegerty Trucking office on the left, Joe O'Hegerty and Ted Joy were standing just outside the door. They both were smiling and waving,

Ted spoke, "There go two legends."

Joe spoke, "That's right, and they're going to show Mark and all the big heads at Can Afford how we used to get things done." Ted nodded his head.

Paul drove up to the fuel pumps at Pensway and Steve, the same Pensway employee that Albert was talking to earlier, was standing beside the Can Afford fuel pump. Steve was smiling as he was looking at the bumper of Paul's truck. Paul shut the engine off. Steve spoke as he approached Paul getting out of the cab, "Paul, you know with that bumper even Armageddon won't stop you."

Paul said, "Yeah, that's what Diesel thinks." Paul pointed to Diesel as he was walking beside Paul's trailer, approaching them.

Diesel said, "Are Can Afford's tanks full?" Steve said, "Yeah, we got 9,000 gallons about three hours ago." Diesel spoke, "Good, because you're going to need it for all those trucks across the street.

Steve replied, "Not me. I'm leaving soon and going to work at South Portland Fire Department," he hesitated, "but first I have to check on Albert's kids to make sure they made it to Maine Med and they're with Michelle in the ICU."

Paul spoke, "Waitress Jenny at Rudy's. I asked Joe O'Hegerty to make sure she gets to Maine Med. With the power being out it's going to be a challenge for us all." Diesel spoke, "Speaking of Albert, have you seen him?" Steve said, "O'Hegerty sent him back to the Produce Market for a second load." Paul spoke loudly, "What? I'll have to talk with Donald about that when I get back. Albert needs to be close to home."

"You know how dispatchers are. If they can get a driver that will run, they'll stick it right to him." Paul said, "Yeah, BUT they crossed the line this time."

Paul started to turn to the left to get into the truck at the same time Steve was pulling the fuel nozzle out of the fuel tank and putting the cap on. Paul got in the truck, started the engine, released the brakes, and drove forward a little so Steve could fuel up the trailer fuel tank. Paul set the parking brake and got out of the truck, walked over to Diesel and said, "I'll call you on the CB when I'm leaving Saugus."

Steve was almost done fueling up the trailer. Diesel said, "I'll keep in touch with you about any changes." Paul got back in his truck and Diesel walked back to his truck. Paul started up his truck, pushed the parking brake, and waved at Steve and drove out from the fuel pumps.

After Paul left Pensway, he looked to the left at the Three Cat Generator Trailers next to some large on the ground transformers (in the warehouse employee parking lot). The largest CAT Generator front top was the number "309". Paul smirked.

Paul came to the stop sign and three antique tractors were coming out of the Main Gate. The first tractor was a Diamond Reo, the second a Brockway, and third was a single sleeper cabover Peterbilt. Paul motioned all three to drive out and get ahead of him, then he grabbed the CB mic. Paul said, "Hey, Smoke, when you get to the end of the dirt lot on your right, turn right, go straight to the end, turn right again and the fuel island will be straight ahead."

The driver of the Diamond Reo "Smoke" replied, "Hey, thanks. I was going to ask. Try to have a safe one, I'll catch up with you tomorrow."

Paul said, "You do the same." He waved the fingers of his

left hand still gripping the steering wheel. A cabover Peterbilt passed Paul, then Paul put his truck in gear, and followed behind. All three antique tractors turned into Pensway's dirt yard and headed toward the fuel island. Paul continued past the O'Hegerty driveway. He made it to Route One.

The police officer directing traffic saw Paul coming and stopped the cars and waved Paul to keep coming. Paul drove out onto Route 1 South and waved as he was shifting up to the next gear. Paul tooted the air horn as he rode by Rudy's Diner. The waitress in the Diner was refilling the glass sugar dispensers in a row on one of the tables. She jumped and spilled sugar on the table and floor.

"Damn you, Paul," she swore.

Paul made it to the through-way to the turnpike and the camera crew was still at the toll booth. The camera man looked at Paul driving toward them. As he put the camera in position to focus on Paul, "Hey, look, was that one of those antique trucks?"

The reporter grabbed his microphone and ordered, "Start recording." The cameraman began recording. The reporter said "This is Dan Rafferty at Exit 45 Maine Turnpike Toll Booth with some good news for Can Afford customers. Can Afford grocery stores will be getting deliveries made for them by a fleet of antique trucks. Here comes one now."

The cameraman smiled and raised his hand with a thumbs up. Paul had a half a smile as he approached the toll booth to pay cash. The toll attendant shook her head with a smile and waved for Paul to drive through. Paul smiled, "Thank you" and continued traveling toward the entrance to the south-bound turnpike.

A few cars, pickup trucks, and a Canadian Fish Trailer Truck were driving south. Two lanes were open for travel. The right lane and the breakdown lanes were cluttered with disabled cars and SUVs. Stewart's Wrecker was towing a Can Afford tractor with a Pensway tractor hauling a Can Afford trailer going north. Paul concentrated on his driving, but the Can Afford driver in the Pensway tractor was staring, mouth open, at Paul heading south.

CHAPTER 9

July 3 at 11:00 AM, Boston Medical Center, Boston.

Boston Medical Center was operating on generator power. Not all patient rooms had electricity. A Hispanic woman in her mid-30s lay in a coma hooked up to life support. The hospital staff was busy responding to patient call buttons lighting up at the nurses' stations. When the power died and transferred over to generator power, the patient alarm system tripped causing patients to panic. This also caused the computer for the life support machine to trip its internal breaker, stopping the function of the machine.

Fifteen minutes later, a nurse came into this patient's room to find the woman had died. The nurse looked at the patient information chart and saw she was an organ donor. The nurse quickly walked out of the patient's room and back to the nurses' station to inform the nurse supervisor. The nurse supervisor was talking to Dr. David Nofrio, a cardiac transplant doctor.

The semi-panicked nurse spoke, "Excuse me, nurse Janet, the female patient in room..."

The nurse supervisor quickly spoke with a pissed-off look on her face, "I am busy talking to Dr. Nofrio."

The nurse said, "She's dead." The nurse supervisor's face

changes as she spoke, "What's the room number and name of the patient?" The nurse spoke, "Room 309, the Hispanic woman marathon runner."

Doctor Nofrio said, "What?! Where's the patient's chart?"

The three of them quickly walk to room 309. Doctor Nofrio asked, "What's this patient's life history?"

The nurse supervisor said, "She has been a marathon runner since high school."

Dr. Nofrio spoke, "Did she have any diseases like AIDS, Hepatitis, Cancer?"

"No, she was very healthy until a car ran a red light and struck her while she was jogging." The nurse continued, "The patient was put on life support, her brain was swelling." Entering the patient's room first, she grabbed the patient's chart and passed it to the nurse supervisor.

Dr. Nofrio said, "What's her blood type?"

The nurse supervisor said, "O Positive" The nurse supervisor continued to look at the chart and confirmed the patient was an organ donor. The nurse supervisor continued, "And, yes, she was an organ donor."

Dr. Nofrio said, "Great! I have a patient in Portland, Maine, at Maine Med, that needs a healthy heart."

As he pointed to the body lying in the bed, "We need to get her into surgery STAT."

Then nurse Janet looked at Dr. Nofrio and said, "Yes, Dr. Nofrio, I will have her ready and at the OR in about five minutes."

Dr. Nofrio said, "I'll go and get everything ready." He quickly walked to the elevator. When it arrived on his floor, he walked quickly to his office and directed "Mona, Call Maine Med Cardiac. Tell them I have a heart for Michelle Hagerthy and she needs to be down here prepped in the OR in three hours."

Mona, the office manager, tried to tell him that the traffic jams may make it impossible. "Yes, but the..."

Dr. Nofrio said, "I don't have time. I'm going to the OR to extract the heart."

Dr. Nofrio quickly left the office to get to the OR.

Mona dialed Maine Med Cardiac. The head nurse of the cardiac ICU answered the phone, "Cardiac ICU."

"Yes, this is Mona at Boston Medical Center of Boston, Dr. Nofrio's office."

The head nurse from Maine Med spoke, a little surprised, "Oh, yes, how may I help you?"

Mona asked, "Do you have a patient by the name of Michelle Hagerthy waiting for a heart transplant?"

The head nurse answered, "Yes, she is in Room 309."

Mona said, "Dr. Nofrio has a matching donor heart for Michelle Hagerthy. The doctor is in the OR now removing the heart from the donor. Dr. Nofrio has told me to inform you that he wants Michelle Hagerthy here at Boston Medical Cardiac OR in three hours."

Now Felicia, Kayla, Marc, and Steve approach the nurses' station as the head nurse was talking, "What?! Does Dr. Nofrio know about the power grid being shut down and all the traffic jams? There is no way we can get Michelle safely down there in that short amount of time or if at all!"

Marc and Steve were talking, Felicia and Kayla looked at each other and said, "What?" Marc and Steve say, "What's going on?"

The head nurse looked up and saw all four of them looking at her with their eyes wide and hands on the counter. The head nurse put her hand over the mic of the phone and spoke, "Dr. Nofrio has a donor heart match for your mother." Then she put one finger to indicate just a minute.

The nurse continued over the phone, "Dr. Nofrio has a better chance at getting up here with the donor heart."

Mona from Dr. Nofrio's office spoke, "I think so too, but he would have to use his own vehicle and still have to deal with traffic jams."

The nurse said, "Surely the Boston Police can help Dr. Nofrio at least out of the city."

Mona said, "I can call the Police Department. I know they are very busy with normal everyday traffic, but today's traffic is very bad."

The nurse said, "My brother is Lieutenant Steve Singer of the Boston Police force. Tell them you need to speak to him directly. When you speak with him, tell him I need him to escort Dr. Nofrio to Maine. If Steve tells you he's too busy, just mention our parents' boat and a water ski ramp on Sebago Lake. He'll do it."

Mona asked, "Ok, what's your brother's name again?" She wrote down his name.

"Call me back when Dr. Nofrio is leaving there." The nurse hung up the phone and stood.

The nurse spoke to all four of them, "Dr. Nofrio is in the OR at Boston Medical Center removing a donor heart for your mother. He wanted us to transport her to BOSTON Medical Center, but that's nearly impossible with all the traffic jams." Steve nodded his head in agreement. The nurse continued speaking, "Dr. Nofrio and the donor heart will have to come here to Maine Med to do the transplant procedure."

Felicia said, "Does my mother know yet?"

The nurse answered, "No, and it's best that she doesn't know until we know for certain that the doctor and donor heart make it here in time."

Felicia said, "What do you mean 'in time'?"

The nurse said, "Well, when Dr. Nofrio removes the heart from the donor he packs the heart in ice. Then he has only a few hours to do the transplant procedure and get the heart pumping again. That's why it is critical for the transit time to be short. Dr. Nofrio is going to need a miracle to get here in time."

Steve said, "I know someone who can help with that miracle."

The nurse supervisor, Felicia, Kayla, and Marc look at Steve and Felicia said, "Who?"

Steve spoke, "Paul Garish."

Felicia spoke, "How? He's retired."

Steve replied, "Paul was hauling a load from the South Portland warehouse to the Can Afford store in Saugus, Mass with his own tractor. All Paul needs to know from the doctor is the time he wants to be here. Paul will get him here ten minutes early."

Felicia spoke, "How can you contact Paul and tell him to pick up Dr. Nofrio?

Steve said, "Diesel over at the Can Afford warehouse has a CB that can reach Connecticut."

Kayla spoke, "What are you waiting for? Go tell Paul to pick up Dr. Nofrio at Boston Medical Center!"

Steve said, "Right."

He spoke to Felicia and looked at all three of them. "Your

father wants you all to stay here. Don't leave."

Marc nodded his head. Felicia and Kayla said, "We won't."

Steve said, "I'll be back later to let you know when Paul and the doctor will get here."

Steve ran from the ICU. He made it to his Jeep in the parking lot across the street from the ER. He drove over the Veteran's Memorial Bridge from Portland to South Portland, then he drove through some side streets taking a shortcut to the Can Afford warehouse. Steve drove into the Warehouse Main Gate then parked beside the Can Afford security SUV. He ran over to the door of the stairs to Can Afford dispatch. He looked at Diesel's tractor hooked up to a trailer at door 66.

He didn't see Diesel anywhere around the truck and trailer, so he went through the door and ran up the stairs to dispatch. Kenny Hewey was talking on the phone to Donald at O'Hegerty. Steve quickly approached the raised counter in front of Kenny and put both his hands on the counter.

Kenny said, "Donald, I'll call you back." He looked at Steve, "What's up?"

Steve spoke with urgency, "I need to talk to Diesel, where is he?"

Kenney answered, "He's driving in the yard with the jockey truck."

Steve said, "This is an emergency, Diesel needs to call Paul on his CB to tell him to pick up Dr. Nofrio at Boston Medical Center."

Kenny spoke with a curious, confused look on his face, "What's going on?"

Just then Diesel was talking to one of the antique truck

drivers on the jockey truck CB, "What trailer number are you looking for?"

Steve and Kenny look at the CB. Kenny stepped over toward the CB and reached for the mic. The antique truck driver replied to Diesel, "8045."

Diesel replied, "Just after the second receiving door."

Kenny grabbed the mic and called for Diesel. "Hey, Diesel, can you come back to dispatch? Steve from Pensway wants to talk to you, he said it's an emergency."

Diesel replied, "I'll be right there." Diesel drove quickly to get back to the dispatch door. Steve started to walk toward the door to the stairs and opened it.

He turned back to look at Kenny, "I'll be back to tell you what's going on after I talk to Paul on Diesel's CB."

Kenny nodded and Steve quickly ran down the stairs.

Just as Diesel pulled the parking brake, Steve stepped outside through the door at the bottom of the stairs. Diesel stepped out of the Yard Jockey truck's back door and stepped down to the ground.

Steve ran up to Diesel and said, "I need to talk to Paul on your CB, it's about Albert's wife."

Diesel said in a frightened voice, "She's not dead?"

Steve spoke as they walked to Diesel's cabover Kenworth tractor. "No, Paul needs to pick-up Michelle's heart transplant doctor, Dr. Nofrio at Boston Medical Center. He has a donor heart that matches Michelle's blood type, O positive."

They made it to the Kenworth. Diesel motioned Steve to get in the passenger door. Then Diesel got in the driver's side, started the engine, and turned on the CB then two other switches for the power booster.

Steve spoke, "I was at the Nurses' station in the Cardiac ICU at Maine Med when Boston Medical Center called. The nurse said that Dr. Nofrio was going to drive from Boston Medical Center to Maine Medical with the donor heart and do the transplant surgery at Maine Med. There's no way the doctor could get to Maine Med in time so I thought with Paul being down there, he would be the doctor's best hope at getting up here."

Diesel nodded in agreement as he grabbed the CB mic, "Hey, Road Boss, you got your ears on?" Diesel spoke to Steve, "Paul has never missed a delivery time." Diesel spoke to the mic again, "Diesel calling Road Boss."

Paul answered back, "What's the matter, you forgot your way back to Maine from Dover?"

Diesel asked, "Where are you now?"

Paul replied, "I'm just pulling out from the dock at Saugus, why? Or better yet, who screwed up from O'Hegerty and they need me to fix it?"

Diesel said, "No, but you need to pick up a priority package and a passenger at BOSTON Medical Center and deliver it to Maine Med."

Paul asked, "What?"

Diesel said, "Dr. Nofrio has a matching donor heart for Michelle, Albert's wife. He is at BOSTON Medical Center and needs to be at Maine Medical in two hours. You and your old workhorse are the best chance at getting him there."

Paul said, "What's he look like?"

Diesel looked at Steve. Steve said, "I guess OR scrubs and carries an ice cooler." Diesel said, "The doctor will be dressed in OR scrubs carrying an ice cooler."

Paul said, "Alright, I'll call you when we're leaving."

Diesel left the truck running, then he and Steve got out of the truck and walked upstairs to the Can Afford dispatch.

Diesel joked as they were getting to the top of the stairs, "I'm going to count all the different paint colors on his bumper when he gets here."

They both laugh as they walk through the doorway at dispatch. Kenny asks, "Alright, what's going on?"

Steve replied, "Earlier Albert was at the fuel island to fuel up his tractor and trailer for a second trip to Boston. He asked me to make sure both his kids and a friend get to Maine Med to be with Michelle, his wife, and their mother. We were standing at the nurses' station and a nurse was on the phone talking to someone at Boston Medical Center in Boston. They have a matching donor heart for Michelle. This heart transplant doctor, Dr. Nofrio, wants Michelle to be transported to Tufts."

Kenny said, "You said earlier that Paul needs to pick up this Dr. Nofrio."

Then Steve continued, "Yeah, I'm getting to that. The Maine Med nurse said there's no way Michelle could safely make the trip, with the way traffic was right now. The person at Boston Medical agreed. Then they started talking about Dr. Nofrio driving with the donor heart to Maine Med. That's when I said to the nurse that Paul could pick-up Dr. Nofrio and get him to Maine Med in time."

CHAPTER 10

July 3 at 12:45 PM, Route 1 Southbound near Tobin Bridge

Paul was bobtailing to Boston Medical Center on Rt. 1, South, passing and zigzagging through cars and trucks and two stopped tour buses. A few car drivers were cut off by Paul, they beeped their horns and waved the famous one finger salute. Paul made it to the Tobin Bridge and saw all the traffic stopped on Northbound Rt. 1. Paul made it to the west end of the Tobin Bridge and turned right at the first exit toward Charlestown. At the traffic light he turned right driving through a red-light powered by solar, causing a Casella garbage truck to jam on its brakes and two taxis rear-ended the truck. Paul continued over the black metal bridge into the North End, Little Italy, driving through intersections, cutting people off. He made it to Durty Nellie's.

A white and blue Chevy Suburban with Boston Medical Center on the driver's door came out of a street on the right. Paul stopped in front of the Suburban and walked around to the driver's door. The driver, Dr. Nofrio rolled the window all the way down and yelled, "Move out of my way, I need to get to Maine, it's an emergency!"

Paul said, "Are you Dr. Nofrio?"

Dr. Nofrio replied, "Yes, and I need to be at Maine Med in

two hours to perform a heart transplant," putting his right hand on the ice cooler.

Paul spoke, "Yeah, for Michelle Hagerthy, but not in that Chevy you won't."

Dr. Nofrio said, "What are you saying?" Just then a one-ton delivery truck got T-boned by a 325i BMW at the intersection behind Paul.

Paul yelled, "I'm saying get in the truck."

Dr. Nofrio looked behind Paul at the accident one last time. Then he took his seat belt off and then removed the seat belt from the cooler. Dr. Nofrio exited the Suburban. Paul walked over to the truck and opened the passenger door. Dr. Nofrio wrinkled his nose and looked at the truck.

Paul asked, "What's the matter?"

Dr. Nofrio handed the cooler to Paul and said, "This truck is so old."

Paul spoke, "So am I. That doesn't mean we're slow. The State Police need a 428 Police Interceptor just to catch up with us and we're not pulling over for any of them."

Dr. Nofrio climbed up and sat in the passenger seat. Paul handed the cooler to Dr. Nofrio.

Paul started to close the passenger door. Dr. Nofrio spoke and put his right hand to stop the door from closing, "I need my medical bag, it's on the floor up front."

Paul went back to the Suburban's driver's side door and reached in and grabbed the medical bag. He returned to the driver's side door of the truck and climbed into the cab, putting the medical bag on the floor between the seats. Paul closed the driver's side door and closed the window, then grabbed the CB mic.

Paul spoke, "Hey Diesel."

Paul waited a few seconds, "Road Boss to Diesel."

Diesel replied, "Go ahead, Paul."

Paul spoke, "The doctor and I are leaving Durty Nellie's now. I'll call again when we get to York."

Diesel replied, "I'll be waiting."

Paul looked at Dr. Nofrio as he hung the CB mic up. Paul spoke, "Paul Garish." Paul put his hand out and the doctor shook his hand.

"David Nofrio."

Paul said, "I'm friends with Albert and Michelle Hagerthy. I used to work with Albert until Can Afford Corp told me I was too old, and I needed to retire."

Dr. Nofrio was holding the cooler in his lap.

Paul said, "Can you put the cooler on the floor beside you?" Paul pointed at the floor space between the seats. Dr. Nofrio put the cooler on the floor. Paul grabbed the shifter handle stick, put the transmission into second gear. "Put your seat belt on. You're in for the ride of your life, not to mention Michelle's."

Dr. Nofrio fastened his seat belt and Paul released the parking brake. Paul completed a quick look around then drove away. Dr. Nofrio held onto the passenger door with his right hand and braced his left hand on the dashboard, with an 'oh shit' look on his face.

Paul asked, "Are you alright?"

Dr. Nofrio answered, "Yeah, I've never done this before."

Paul said, "That's what she said till the bed broke." Paul turned the truck around to head back the same way he came.

Paul drove back over the metal bridge and up to the traffic

light. The garbage truck had moved forward leaving a 40-foot space between the two smashed taxi cabs and the back of the garbage truck. The two taxi drivers were yelling at the garbage truck driver behind the truck. Paul looked at them. The garbage truck driver pointed at Paul's truck as he slowly drove by. The garbage truck driver looked at the name above the back window of Paul's truck, In purple letters "MR GREEN,"

Paul turned left into the 40-foot space to the Tobin Bridge off ramp. One of the taxis was partly blocking the ramp.

Dr. Nofrio spoke a little loudly, "You're going the wrong way."

Paul said, "I know." Dr. Nofrio said, "There's not enough room."

Paul spoke, "I'll make room." Then Paul crashed the taxi into the concrete barricade, then stopped and backed up. Paul continued, "I've always wanted to do that to a Boston Taxicab." He continued driving the wrong way onto the Tobin Bridge. The two taxi drivers started to run after Paul and the doctor. The garbage truck driver got in his truck and drove away. Paul pulled the left one of two pull cables at the center of the cab's roof. The air horn on the roof blasted and Dr. Nofrio jumped a little. Paul turned on the flashers and the headlights on high beams. They make it across the Tobin Bridge with a few near misses with a few cars and an Asian produce truck. Dr. Nofrio's eyes were opened wide, and his body tensed against the back of the seat.

Paul spoke as they arrived in Chelsea, MA and Route 1 north lane and south lane drew closer to each other. The traffic was stopped on Route 1 North. "That's why we're going the wrong way." They continued headed North into Revere and began to slow down at Logan Airport off ramp traffic circle. Paul pulled the air horn again. The doctor didn't jump this time. Paul spoke, "Hey, you didn't jump this time." The doctor still had a stunned look on his face.

They make it to the T-Rex Mini Golf Course where Route 99 and Route 1 split. Now there were three lanes, not two, and Paul started driving faster on the right (which was beside the median guardrail). A Saugus cop was in the Square One Mall parking lot. The officer was outside of the patrol car looking at Route 1 traffic. He heard and looked south on Route 1. He watched Paul and the doctor drive by going north in the southbound lanes. The officer said, "What the hell?" The officer quickly returned to his cruiser, turned on the blue lights, and drove onto Route 1 going north in the southbound lane as he started chasing Paul and the doctor. Then he requested backup on the radio.

Paul arrived at Papa Gino's Pizza, and quickly pulled into the parking lot. Paul warned, "Hang on."

Paul drove out back of the restaurant to the grocery dock area of the Saugus Can Afford store and hooked up to the trailer he had dropped earlier.

Dr. NoFrio asked, "What are you doing?"

Paul replied, "We need the extra weight for traction."

The doctor said, "We don't have snow in July."

Paul spoke, "Trust me, we need the weight. I'll only be a minute."

Just as Paul got out of the truck, he saw the cop car going north with the blue lights flashing and siren sounding. Then he hooked up the air lines and cranked up the landing gear. Paul got back in the truck and said, "Now the real fun begins." He fastened his seat belt, put the transmission into gear, and released the trailer brakes.

They drove onto Route 1 South and continued driving north. They drove by the Christmas Tree shop. The cruiser was at the gas station, the officer was inside the store asking the store attendant if he had seen a truck driving the wrong way. The attendant was shaking his head no. Then Paul and the doctor drove by, but the officer was looking at the attendant, not Route One.

At the register there was a "cash only: sign. The attendant opened his eyes wide and nodded his head and pointed to Route 1. The officer looked at Route 1 and said, "Ah, shit!" He quickly ran outside to get into the cruiser. He saw an older minivan blocking his only way to drive forward, and he couldn't back up because of the concrete barricade.

The officer said, "Damn it." He walked back inside and asked the attendant, "Do you know who owns that minivan?"

The attendant made an 'I don't know' look and shook his head. Just then, an old man came out of the restroom, walking slowly with his cane and toilet paper stuck to his shoe.

The officer saw two people getting chips and two sodas from the glass door refrigerator. The officer walked up to them and said, "I need you to move your minivan right now." The old man was walking out the front door. The two people say, "We don't have a minivan." The store attendant pointed outside toward the old man approaching the minivan. The officer quickly walked outside and to the driver's door of the minivan. The old man was getting into the driver's seat with a bit of a struggle. The officer spoke, "I need you, sir, to move your vehicle right NOW."

The old man was startled and dropped the keys on the floor of the minivan. The old man said, "Oh, you shocked me. Yes, I'll move as soon as I find my keys." The old man reached down to the floor and felt around, finally finding them. The officer was already in the cruiser and had the engine running. His finger was on the switch to turn the blue lights on. The officer grimaced and groaned. Then the old man started the minivan. He looked around, put the transmission into drive, and moved forward. The officer turned on the blue lights and the siren and drove north onto southbound Route One.

The officer drove out into oncoming traffic causing one car to jam on their brakes and was rear-ended by another car. While the officer was getting free of the old man's minivan, Paul drove off the Lynnfield onramp then turned right to drive over Route 1 and drove straight toward Lynne Route 129 and Swampscott.

The doctor asked, "Where are we going now?"

Paul replied, "You'll see."

Paul continued driving about a quarter mile to a traffic circle. He entered the circle and exited the circle on the other side of the sign I-95 North.

The doctor said, "Well, I learned something new."

Paul, with half a grin, looked at the doctor.

Paul and the doctor look ahead and see traffic stopped in the far-left lanes. The doctor said, "That doesn't look good." Paul stayed to the right and got to Route 128/I-95 and saw the traffic stopped for Route 128 which splits to the left.

Paul continued in the right lane for I-95 North.

Now, Paul's timing worked out. The Saugus police officer wasn't having much luck. He continued north on Route 1 in the southbound lanes. The officer made it to the only traffic light on Route 1, just after the Sonic Restaurant. A state trooper was standing in the middle of the reverse direction intersection. The Saugus cop stopped and asked the state trooper, "Did you see a huge truck pulling a Can Afford trailer driving north in the southbound lane?"

The state trooper replied, "No. Where was the last place you saw this truck?"

The Saugus cop spoke, "The Christmas Tree Shop. How can a truck that big just disappear?"

The state trooper said, "Maybe it was one of those phantom ghost trucks."

The Saugus cop spoke, "No, I know I'm not going crazy. He must have gotten off at 129."

The Saugus cop turned around and drove south on Route 1. The cop waved at the state trooper as the trooper stopped southbound vehicles. The state trooper waved back. The Saugus cop again turned on the blue lights and the siren and sped away.

Paul and the doctor were driving past the exit to 114, Paul asked the doctor, "How much time do we have left?"

Dr. Nofrio looked at his watch and replied with a bit of uncertainty on his face as he looked at the speedometer, "An hour and twenty minutes."

The speedometer read 50 mph. Paul looked at the speedometer, then turned on the power booster switch on Channel 19 for the CB and increased the volume, then grabbed the mic.

Paul spoke, "Attention to all you drivers headed north on 95. This is Paul Garish or Road Boss, as some of you may know me. I have an urgent emergency request. I need to be at

Maine Medical Center in a little over one hour from now. I cannot miss my delivery time. My freight is a heart transplant doctor with an organ donor's heart. So, if you could open a fast travel lane to help another fellow truck driver's wife live, I know he and their kids would really appreciate it."

Paul put the mic back on the radio. Dr. Nofrio said, "Do you think that will help?"

Paul said, "Give them a minute."

Some other driver said, "Hey Paul, are you the same Road Boss that drove for O'Hegerty Trucking?"

Paul grabbed the mic and replied, "Yeah, who am I talking to?"

The driver said, "Jimmy. My uncle was Chuck Badard, rest his soul. He used to tell me stories about you. Anyway, three French Transport drivers and I will help open up a clear shot to Maine."

Paul said, "Hey, thanks a lot, Albert, another O'Hegerty driver, he and his family will be eternally grateful."

While driving North on I-495, Albert heard Paul and turned up the volume on his CB.

Jimmy said, "What yardstick are you at and what are you driving?" Paul looked to the right and saw mile marker 73.5.

Paul said, "We're at 73.8 yardstick in a Green autocar with a Can Afford trailer."

Jimmy spoke as he looked at a mile marker, "Yeah, we're about a mile ahead of you. We'll get the middle-left lane open." All four Peterbilt trailer trucks accelerated and blew their airhorns. Cars and a couple of pick-ups with Bass boats moved to the right.

Jimmy said, "Hey, Paul, where are you now?"

"At your back door."

Jimmy looked in his driver's door mirror and his speedometer was at 75 mph. Jimmy moaned to himself, "Holy shit!

Then Jimmy spoke into the mic, "Damn. Now I know why they call you Road Boss." A short pause then Jimmy continued speaking, "Paul, how fast does that old horse go?"

"Double nickels times two."

Jimmy whispered to himself, "Damn," then to the mic, "We can take you up 95 all the way to Portsmouth, then we're going up 16 to Dover."

Paul spoke, "We're right behind you," and looked at Dr. Nofrio.

Then Jimmy spoke to the other French Transport drivers, "You heard him boys, take this train to full speed. Hey, drivers on Northbound 95 north of mile marker 77, we need your help to keep the middle-left lane open."

A Heartland Express truck replied, "Jimmy, I'm a Heartland driver about three miles ahead of you. I can only do seventy-two, but I'll do what I can. There was a JP Noonan driver ahead of me, I know he can go faster."

The JP Noonan driver said, "Yeah, that's right. Kenworth with a Canadian Moose catcher. This king of the road knows how to push 4-wheelers out of the way."

Paul said, "Lucky 7 will get us almost to the Portsmouth/Kittery Bridge."

Dr. Nofrio spoke, "Let's hope that luck gets up through the New Hampshire Toll Booth."

Paul and the doctor look at each other. Paul raised his right eyebrow and nodded his head and spoke, "Yeah."

Now the Noonan driver drove into the middle-left lane,

then he directed, "Hey, Heartland driver, get behind me to keep some four-wheelers from following me, I'll keep it at seventy-two till French and Road Boss catch up."

They made it to about a mile before the Newport exit and traffic started slowing down. The Noonan driver said, "Hey, French driver, Jimmy, the road is getting constipated by the Newport exit."

Jimmy said, "Yeah, we're catching up to you. Close to a half mile. Hey boys, put it on three stage. Paul, we're backing down."

Paul stepped on the brakes and a space opened between the last French Transport trailer dump, and Paul's Green autocar. Then a Fast Supercrete empty flatbed trailer truck changed lanes and cut out in front of Paul and the doctor. Paul spoke, "Hold on." Paul locked up the brakes.

Dr. Nofrio asked in a whisper, "What the hell is he doing?"

Paul grabbed the CB mic, "Supercrete, your eyes and mirror broken?"

The Fast Supercrete driver didn't reply. Paul and the doctor looked at each other.

Paul asked, "You and the heart alright, Doc?"

With both hands on the cooler, Dr. Nofrio breathed, "Yes. We're not going to make it."

Paul's face muscles tightened then he looked to the median and saw a short dirt crossroad used as a police turnaround just after the Fast Supercrete truck. Paul grabbed the CB mic and said, "Hey, driver in the caboose of the French train, can you move ahead about a truck length and a half?"

The French Transport driver replied, "Well, I can't move forward, but I can change lanes." So, the French Transport driver pulled the air horn and drove or forced the vehicles to the right of him either to stop or move to the right. The French Transport driver made a complete lane change. Then the Fast Supercrete moved ahead about thirty feet and stopped, leaving plenty of space between his truck and the French Transport truck.

Then Paul pulled the left cable blowing the air horn. The Fast Supercrete driver pulled his parking brake. Paul put the transmission in gear and started to drive into the median. Now the Fast Supercrete driver released his brakes and drove his tractor to the left, blocking Paul.

Dr. Nofrio said, "What an asshole." Then he grabbed the right cable, and Paul spoke, "Not that one."

Paul put his right hand up under Dr. Nofrio's left hand to keep the doctor from pulling down the right cable. Then Paul grabbed the CB mic, "Hey, Supercrete driver, what's your problem? I don't want to get ahead of you, I just need to get to the dirt cop turn around." The driver extended his left arm from his window and gave Paul the middle finger.

Paul muttered, "That's it, no more Mister Nice Guy. Hey, French drivers, you need to move ahead, I need to move some shitcrete that's in my way."

They moved ahead, Paul put the power divider in gear then backed up about fifteen feet, then put the transmission in second gear. Then Paul steered to the left, drove forward, then to the right to T-Bone the Fast Supercrete trailer, forcing the Fast Supercrete trailer truck to jackknife while pushing the right front and side of the tractor into the concrete barricade in the median just north of the turn-around.

Paul grabbed the CB mic, "How do you like that crete dickhead?" Paul disengaged the power divider then backed up and turned the steering wheel to drive into the southbound lanes and drove north.

Paul spoke on the CB, "Hey, Jimmy and all you other drivers, thanks for your help, but we can't wait." Paul put down the mic and started driving north. As they passed by the Fast Supercrete driver getting out of his smashed-up tractor, Dr. Nofrio gave him the middle finger. The engine roared and black exhaust smoke puffed from two smokestacks as Paul shifted through the gears and blasted away. Paul turned on his flashers with headlights on high beams. As they drove north in the southbound lane, the oncoming traffic quickly moved out of their way. State troopers on the northbound side of I-95 were watching Paul and the doctor drive by. One of the troopers ran to his cruiser and talked on the police radio to inform other troopers to stop Paul from driving the wrong way.

CHAPTER 11

July 3 at 2:00 PM, Northbound I-95, New Hampshire

Albert and Gonzo see Paul and Doctor Nofrio drive by them. So, Albert and Gonzo drove over into the left lane going north on I-95. Then they both turned into a DOT cross-road so they could drive north in the southbound lane. They had their flashers on and headlights on high beams while driving at 68 mph, as fast as the engine would allow them. Some oncoming vehicles going south moved over to their right and looked at both of them like they were crazy.

Paul and Dr. Nofrio were going through the Hampton Toll Booth EasyPass lane at about 85 mph. On the north end of the EasyPass lane blocking the roadway were orange cones and orange plastic barrels to keep the southbound traffic from not paying a toll. EasyPass doesn't work with no electricity. A New Hampshire state trooper sat in his Chrysler cruiser parked beside the concrete barricade wall and the cash toll booths. North of the southbound toll gates, the state trooper looked as Paul and the doctor drove by. He immediately turned the cruiser around. With blue lights and headlights flashing and the siren blaring, the state trooper chased after Paul and the doctor.

Paul looked in the driver's rearview mirror and saw the

state trooper chasing them. Paul grabbed the mic, "Hey, New Hampshire state trooper, you got your ears on?"

The New Hampshire state trooper replied, "Yes, I do. Are you the driver hauling the Can Afford trailer north in the southbound?"

Paul spoke, "Yes, this is an emergency. My passenger will explain."

Paul handed the mic to Dr. Nofrio, "You tell him, I've got to drive."

Looking at the oncoming traffic going south, swerving and moving over toward the breakdown lane away from Paul's truck, Dr. Nofrio grabbed the mic and spoke as he looked at Paul. "What do I say?"

"Just tell him who you are, what we are doing, and where we are going. And tell him how much time we've got left."

Dr. Nofrio nodded his head and spoke into the mic, "I'm Dr. David Nofrio, lead heart transplant physician of Boston Medical Center. I have with me a donor heart. We need to be at Maine Med," with a slight hesitation as he looked at his watch, "just under an hour from now, for me to do the operation."

The state trooper said, "Really, I can't say I've heard them all, but this is a new one."

Paul looked at Dr. Nofrio and reached for the mic. The doctor gave the mic back to Paul.

Paul spoke tersely, "Listen to me, Barney, a friend of mine's wife needs this heart. If you and your fellow troopers try slowing me down, it is just going to piss me off. You don't want me mad behind the wheel of this truck."

Dr. Nofrio nodded his head yes.

Paul looked ahead and saw a front-end loader and a wrecker

trying to get the trash trailer truck back on its wheels. Paul said, "Shit, I forgot about that accident." Now Paul stepped on the brakes. As he was slowing down the state trooper drove up to the right side of Paul and the doctor. The cooler sat on the doctor's lap, blocking the mirror from Paul to see the right side of the truck. On the window side of the cooler written in big letters was "BMC Donor Heart."

The state trooper looked up at the cooler. Just then, Dr. Nofrio looked down at the state trooper looking up. The doctor pointed at the words, "See!"

The state trooper put up his thumb. He stepped on the accelerator and passed Paul and the doctor to clear the roadway ahead by the rolled over trash truck.

The state trooper and Paul drove by the trash truck. Just after they make it past the trash truck, a car rear ended a dump truck dispatched to clean up the garbage. The state trooper said, "Hey, driver, I have to stop. Good luck!"

Paul said, "Thank you."

Paul accelerated in the southbound left side, because there were orange cones to his left to keep southbound traffic from traveling in that lane due to the truck roll-over. Paul and the doctor made it to the TA truck stop on their left. Paul looked straight ahead and noticed the traffic flow driving south was thinning out.

Paul said, "Something is wrong."

"What do you mean?" asked Dr. Nofrio.

"There should be more cars and trucks coming south."

Dr. Nofrio said, "That's good for us, we can get into Maine faster." Just then they drove under an overpass and looked ahead to see a tri-axle wrecker, an airport high pressure fire truck, and two Clean Harbor hazmat trucks blocking the entire southbound lanes.

Dr. Nofrio said, "Oh shit."

The wrecker driver and two Clean Harbor drivers were putting on their hazmat suits as they saw Paul driving toward them. They dropped their suits and they waved their hands above their heads making an "x" sign and started running toward Paul and the doctor.

Paul drove up to them and stopped. The wrecker driver said, "The bridge is closed north and southbound."

"Why?" Paul demanded.

One of the Clean Harbor men said, "There was a chlorine gas tanker coming south at the top of the bridge with a steel I-beam sticking into the tank leaking chlorine gas. The entire bridge was evacuated."

Paul asked, "Is the northbound side clear?"

The other Clean Harbor man answered, "All three lanes are full of abandoned cars and trucks. Nobody can be on the bridge North or South. We have to wait for the chlorine gas to stop leaking."

Paul looked at Dr. Nofrio and the cooler in his lap. The doctor had a disappointed look on his face, "You gave it one hell of a shot."

Paul and the doctor look at each other. Paul has a memory flashback of his wife laying in a hospital bed. Paul entered the patient's room as the doctor and nurse pulled the sheet over his wife's face. Paul's two sons sat in chairs next to the wall and they were both crying. Paul was wearing his O'Hegerty uniform.

Just then the Autocar cab shook a little, as another New

Hampshire State Trooper's voice came from outside the driver's window, "Officer Hagerty informed me of your situation, so I can escort you both up Route 16 into Dover all the way to Berwick, Maine."

Paul looked at the northbound lanes of Route I-95 and saw two NH DOT dump trucks and a Portsmouth cop car blocking the three travel lanes. Paul then looked at the state trooper, "We don't have time for that. I need you to tell that Portsmouth cop to move his car or lose it!" Paul, stone-faced, put the transmission into gear and the state trooper quickly got off the truck.

Paul drove south on I-95 to a access road between north and south lanes about a quarter mile south.

Dr. Nofrio asked, "Where are we going?"

As Paul made a wide right turn to turn left into the crossroad, he said, "I drove my life into hell, and I've been in hell since my wife died. I'll be damned if Albert is going to. So, I'm driving back to Maine, and nothing is going to slow me down."

Paul drove into the northbound side of I-95 and came to a stop after the trailer was straight behind the tractor. Paul flipped the power divider switch to lock the two drive axles into four-wheel drive. Paul rolled the truck forward to make sure the axles locked into gear. Paul looked ahead at the state trooper talking to the Portsmouth cop.

Paul spoke, "Now when we get to the beginning of the bridge your door window needs to be all the way up. Then take a deep breath and hold it. Close your eyes tight. I'll tell you when to breathe and open your eyes." Paul pulled a pair of ear plugs out of his shirt pocket and as he spoke, Paul put them in his ears. "But right now, you need to plug your ears."

Paul put his right hand up to the right cable above the dashboard, Paul spoke very loudly, "Are you ready?"

Dr. Nofrio turned his head toward Paul to show his fingers plugging his ears as he nodded his head. Paul pulled the right cable. A train horn sounded, and the doctor jumped, and the state trooper and the Portsmouth cop jumped, then looked at Paul's truck. Paul started driving toward them. When Paul shifted to fifth gear, he pulled on the train horn again then the Portsmouth cop quickly moved his cruiser out of the way just as Paul drove through.

Paul looked at the speedometer then he looked at the cars and trucks with their doors open, left abandoned. Paul stepped on the throttle and shifted the transmission, stepped on the throttle again, bringing the truck speed up to 60 mph. Black smoke blew out of the exhaust stacks both times he stepped on it. Paul looked at the top of the bridge to see the chlorine gas blowing across the northbound lanes. Wind from the North was blowing the gas cloud across all the travel lanes and the abandoned vehicles. The cloud was moving to the side of the bridge toward the ocean. Paul reached for the horn cable again and pulled on the cable making it sound like a train was coming through.

Paul looked at the speedometer and it was at 68 mph, then he looked at the RPMs and they were almost maxed out. Paul then drove to the left and straddled the far-left lane and the middle lane. They were about a hundred yards from the abandoned cars and Paul said, "Hold on!"

The doctor held tight to the cooler with his right hand and braced his left hand against the dashboard. Dr. Nofrio's face wrinkled into a stressed, fearful, 'oh shit' look. Paul was gripping the steering wheel with both hands. Paul's face muscles tightened, and his eyes squinted a little. He first hit the left car and then the car on the right crushing the right rear of the left car and the left rear of the right. Both cars lunged forward, rear ending the cars ahead of them. The cars on the left were pushed to the concrete barricade wall that separated the north and southbound lanes.

The cars on the left hit the short wall and rolled over onto the southbound lanes, just like an angled snowplow. The cars on the right get crushed and thrown to the right, smashing into the trucks and campers in the right travel lane.

They made it to the beginning of the bridge. As they started going uphill toward the top of the bridge, Paul cautioned, "Hold your breath!" Paul looked at the speedometer at 58 mph. Paul down shifted and black smoke rolled from the exhaust. The speed of the truck approached 60 mph. Paul yelled as they approached about one hundred feet from the chlorine cloud, "Close your eyes!"

Paul held his breath then squinted his eyes. A Chevy pick-up was in the left lane just before the chlorine truck. Paul accelerated, pushing the pick-up over the median wall, hitting the I-Beam, breaking it free from the tank truck.

They passed the tank truck and the state of Maine State Line sign. Paul looked forward at the abandoned cars he saw at the Maine side end of the bridge. There was an open highway going North.

Paul looked at the driver's side door mirror to see the chlorine gas cloud getting bigger and thicker because the I-Beam was no longer partially plugging the hole. The truck made it to the downhill Maine side of the bridge. They gained speed and Paul shifted up a gear then looked at both left and right mirrors to see the chlorine cloud was behind the trailer. Paul opened his door window a little and does a little sniff. Then opened the window fully and also opened his eyes.

Paul spoke, "You can open your eyes and breathe now. Open your window, too."

Dr. Nofrio looked into the passenger door mirror and saw the chlorine cloud going through the cars and trucks, then over the edge of the bridge. Paul looked forward to the end of the bridge and beyond. There were no more cars and trucks going North. Paul asked the doctor, "How much time do we have?"

The doctor replied, as he looked at his watch, "Forty minutes," then he looked at the speedometer. Paul saw the doctor looking at the truck speed, 68 mph. Paul said, "You can put the cooler on the floor. I need to see the trailer in your mirror."

Dr. Nofrio placed the cooler on the floor between the seats. After the doctor pushed the cooler against the back of the cab, he looked at the speedometer, 78 mph, as they drove by the off ramp to the Visitor Center.

Paul saw two Maine DOT trucks driving in the right lane, coming out of the Visitor Center. He pulled on the left cable and tooted the air horn once. They continued driving in the left lane as they passed the off ramp for the York truck scales. The speedometer was maxed out at 85 mph.

Paul warned, "As we get to the toll booth let me know if any cars are coming down the on ramp and hold the cooler tight against the back wall." Paul pulled the left cable air horn, then pushed the clutch to the floor and disengaged the power divider, and drove through the wide load toll booth at 45 mph. Paul grabbed the CB mic, "Hey, Diesel, you out there?"

July 3 at 2:20 PM, Can Afford Warehouse, South Portland

In front of dock door 70, Ralph Morse, Diesel, and Steve, are standing on the ground between 146 tractor O'Hegerty single sleeper W900 Kenworth and Diesel's double bunk cabover Kenworth. Diesel was telling Ralph about some of the antique trucks and the drivers standing at the dispatch desk. They were watching Bob Cyr inform Ron LaFlute that he was not in charge anymore. Diesel, Ralph, and Steve stopped laughing when they heard Paul speak on the CB in Diesel's truck.

Diesel quickly walked to the driver's side of the cabover, climbed up into the truck and grabbed the CB mic, "Go ahead Road Boss."

Paul said, "We just went through the York tolls. We'll be at the 295-toll booth in 30 minutes. Can you make sure there was a clear path on 295? We're going straight to Maine Med."

Ralph responded, "I'll clear out the 295-toll booth."

Diesel added, "Yeah, Ralph said he'd clear-out the toll booth. Steve from Pensway and I will take care of 295 and the streets to Maine Med." During the time Diesel was talking, Paul was shifting the transmission and gaining speed.

Paul spoke into the CB mic, "Great, can you do me one more favor and move down to 19? Tell every trucker going north on 95 to keep one lane open. The doctor and I will be coming through at a Ben Franklin and Abraham Lincoln?"

Dr. Nofrio looked at Paul with a puzzled look on his face. Then the doctor's eyes opened wide, "Really?"

Paul nodded his head, "I don't miss a delivery time," and reset the mic in its cradle.

Back at Can Afford Warehouse. Diesel spoke to Steve, "Can you run upstairs and tell Hewey he needs to get a Can Afford driver to be a yard slut because we need to go right now."

Steve ran to the door for dispatch and ran up the stairs and slammed opened the door to dispatch.

Kenny looked at Steve as he barged through the doorway.

Kenny said, "What's up?"

"Paul and a heart transplant doctor are on their way up 95 headed to Maine Med. Diesel, Ralph, and I are going to clear a path on 295. Diesel said you'll have to get a Can Afford driver to be a yard slut."

Kenny spoke with a confused and surprised look on his face, "What, how did Paul make it back here so fast with a heart transplant doctor?"

Steve spoke quickly as he was about to grab the door handle to the stairs, "Albert's wife needs another heart and Paul was making sure she got it. This doctor has a donor heart with him. I got to go!"

Steve ran down the stairs and pushed open the door. Then he ran to the passenger's side, climbed into the seat, then closed the door.

Diesel asked, "We all set?"

Steve nodded his head and pointed forward as he was trying to catch his breath.

Ralph drove out through the main gate and Diesel drove

right behind him. Diesel turned his CB to Channel 19, turned on the power booster then spoke into the mic, "Breaker one nine to all you drivers coming North on 95 from York, Maine, to Portland, Maine. A friend of mine, Road Boss, is helping with a medical emergency. He has a donor heart and a transplant doctor as his freight that he needs to deliver to Maine Medical in about thirty minutes. So, if you could help keep one lane open, Road Boss is driving a big old Autocar pulling a Can Afford trailer. A O'Hegerty driver's wife needs that heart."

A driver of an old red Mack with a Can Afford trailer driving North on 95 between the Wells and Kennebunk exits, grabbed his CB mic, "Hey Road Boss, this is Diggity Dog and I'm at yard stick # 22, let me know when you're getting close, and I'll clear a path for you."

Paul handed the mic to the doctor, "Here, tell him we are at mile marker 20, two miles south of the Mack and we'll be where he was—Paul looked quickly at the speedometer with the needle at the bottom of the gauge—in about a minute."

Now all the drivers going north turned up the volume on their CBs.

Doctor Nofrio spoke into the CB mic, "We're at mile marker 20 and we'll catch up to you in about a minute."

All the drivers going north are looking at the sides of the highway for mile markers and their rear-view mirrors. A couple of drivers say, "Holy shit, he's moving!"

CHAPTER 12

July 3 at 2:35 AM, Northbound I-95 near Kennebunk Exit

Back to Paul and the doctor. Paul spoke, "See the cigarette ash tray? Open it, there is a new pair of earplugs. Put them in your ears, you're gonna have to blow the big horn."

The doctor inserted the ear plugs in his ears.

Paul looked ahead and saw the Can Afford trailer being pulled by the red Mack. Paul said, "Pull the horn."

The driver of the Mack was in the left lane, heard the train air horn, and looked into his driver's side door mirror.

The Mack driver muttered, "Damn," then put on his right blinker. There was an older Subaru station wagon in the middle lane just behind the back of the trailer. Now the Subaru driver accelerated to about the middle of the trailer and stayed there. The Mack driver spoke, "What an asshole," then he looked in the driver's side mirror and saw Road Boss getting closer.

The Mack driver spoke through clenched teeth, "I hate Subarus," as he moved over to the middle lane. The Subaru driver beeped his horn, looking at the trailer getting much closer to him. Then he quickly changed lanes to the right where a Maine Turnpike dump truck was parked. The Subaru swerved to the right off the highway into a small wetland swamp. Paul raced by and the doctor spoke on the CB, "Thank you."

Now Paul and the doctor crested the top of the hill just before the Kennebunk truck stop. Paul said, "Pull the horn."

The doctor pulled the horn three times, like a train was coming. At the Kennebunk truck stop there were a lot of people with broken down vehicles and trucks.

Five Can Afford trucks were broken down. They heard the train horn. They all turned their heads and looked south at the highway.

One driver yelled, "What the hell? There are no train tracks around here."

Just then, Paul and the doctor came into view and drove past the truck stop. Two of the drivers swore, "Holy shit! He's moving!"

Another Can Afford driver said, "That trailer has never gone that fast."

Another driver said, "That was the fastest any Can Afford trailer has ever gone." The first driver asked, "How fast do you think he's going?"

The second driver answered, "At least 90."

All five drivers agreed, nodding their heads and saying, "Yup," as they looked north on 95. Then the doctor blew the train horn again.

All the trucks going north are in the far-left lane. As they see the Autocar, all trucks move to the right into the middle lane. In the far-left lane Paul and the doctor drove past them all.

Ralph, Diesel, and Steve at the entrance of the 295-toll booth lanes. They are trying to move a Cadillac Escalade from the right lane toll booth when they hear Dr. Nofrio on the

CB, "Breaker one nine for Diesel, Road Boss and I are crossing the Saco River Bridge."

Ralph, Diesel, and Steve are pushing the Escalade when they hear the doctor on Ralph's CB, Ralph said, "Screw it, we ain't got time for this!"

Ralph ran to his W900, got in the cab, drove through the southbound toll booth and made a U-turn and drove behind the Escalade.

Diesel directed Ralph closer as Steve got into the driver's side of the Escalade. Ralph pushed the Escalade onto the shoulder and grass. Then Ralph backed up and parked where the Escalade had been.

Ralph got out of the W900 and walked in front of the truck to meet Diesel walking toward Ralph.

Ralph spoke, "There, that was much easier. Diesel, I'll stay here to keep this lane closed till Paul gets here. You and Steve go check out the rest of the way." Diesel nodded his head, then he and Steve ran to the cabover. Ralph yelled over to them, "Let me know if you need my help."

Diesel gave him a thumbs up gesture. Diesel and Steve climbed into the cabover and sped away, going north on 295 with exhaust smoke blowing out both smokestacks.

Ralph walked back to the W900 and as he opened the driver's side door, he saw a small line of cars and a couple of Jeeps in the right lane coming to the cash toll booth. Ralph got in the truck and grabbed the CB mic and spoke, "Hey, Road Boss, this is Ralph at the 295 off ramp toll booth."

Paul told the doctor to reply, "Tell him to go ahead."

The doctor said, "Go ahead."

Ralph continued speaking, "Paul, when you get off the exit

to I-295 get in the break-down lane, there's a line of cars in the travel lane. Let me know when you get on the off ramp, I'm in the right toll booth. I'll move when you get here."

Paul said, "Tell him ok."

The doctor said, "Ok."

Ralph started the W900, rolled the driver's side window down and left the door open. He watched the cars pay their tolls.

Diesel and Steve were driving on 295 northbound at the straight stretch between the tidal water and end of Portland Airport runway. The traffic was moving about 40 - 45 mph.

Steve said, "Wow, it's actually moving normally, but it does kinda suck."

Diesel spoke with a tightened eyebrow, "What's that supposed to mean?"

Steve said, "Well, I was looking forward to watching you and Ralph push the 4-wheelers out of the way."

Diesel drove off at exit 5. A raised paved island separated the off ramp from 295N. Diesel drove up onto the long island and stopped, then pulled the parking brake. Diesel grabbed the CB mic and said, "Hey, Ralph, Steve and I are at exit 5 off ramp. Traffic was moving about 45 mph and the off ramp was clear."

Ralph replied, "Good, let's hope it stays that way."

Paul and the doctor were at the I-295 off ramp going 75 mph. The doctor pulled the right horn cable.

Ralph heard the train horn. Ralph spoke into the CB mic as he closed the driver's side door of his truck, "The Boss has arrived." Ralph released the parking brake and put the transmission in gear. Ralph looked into the driver's side mirror and saw the Autocar driving fast in the travel lane and moving to the breakdown lane.

The doctor pulled the horn again.

Ralph drove out of the toll booth in fifth gear spinning the drive axle tires driving into the left lane to hold back the cars leaving the toll booth.

Paul approached the right toll booth and one of two Fast & Furious tour cars in the cash line started to drive up to the right toll booth. Paul rear ended the car and the air scoop fin broke off the car and stabbed into the radiator of the Autocar. The car then skidded into the rear end of the Escalade.

Paul drove on with steam billowing out and over the hood of the truck.

Dr. Nofrio said, "Oh shit."

Paul spoke as he looked at the engine temperature gauge, 210 degrees, "We're almost there." Paul looked at the speedometer, 65 mph.

Ralph followed behind Paul. Ralph asked over the CB, "Did you blow a hose?"

Paul replied, "No, I think something broke off the dumb ass in the Fast & Furious car and hit the radiator."

Ralph spoke, "Well, I'm sure that dumb ass is furious now. Your old Autocar was faster."

Paul looked at the temperature gauge again, it was 220 degrees. Paul and the doctor were driving on the overpass with the Pape Chevrolet dealership on their left. Paul saw the traffic slowing down and he slowed to 45 mph. The steam was rolling out from the front of the truck and over the windshield.

Ralph spoke on the CB, "Hey Diesel, How's the traffic?"

Diesel said, "295 traffic was still moving, but down by Denny's on Congress Street there are some cars stopped, but a Portland police cruiser just showed up."

Paul and the doctor passing the northbound on-ramp from Route 1, South Portland.

At the same time Joe O'Hegerty and the waitress from Rudy's Diner are driving down the 295 North on ramp in Paul's 1932 Ford Phaeton license plate 309. The waitress spoke, "Is that Paul? Why's that smoke coming out of the front of his truck?"

Joe said, "That's not smoke, it's antifreeze, he must have blown a hose or something."

Paul and the doctor make it to the off ramp where Diesel was parked. Just as Paul drove onto the off ramp the engine temperature hit 230 degrees and the engine shut down.

Dr. Nofrio spoke with a look of fear, "What happened to the engine?"

Paul pointed at the engine gauge reading 232 degrees and Paul said, "The engine shuts down when the engine temperature gets to 230 degrees." Paul continued driving the Autocar on the off ramp and up onto the island where Diesel was parked.

Paul stopped behind Diesel's truck.

Dr. Nofrio looked at his watch and said, "I've got to be at Maine Med in five minutes."

Diesel and Steve get out of the cabover and started walking toward Paul and the doctor.

Paul said, "Diesel, can take you the rest of the way."

Paul opened the driver's side door and got out and walked to the front of the Autocar and looked at the metal fin stuck into the radiator.

Diesel walked up and said, "You and the old beast made it."

Paul spoke, "Not quite, the doctor needs to be at Maine Med in five minutes. Can you take him the rest of the way?"

Diesel spoke, "Yes, (cuss) I will. Hey Steve, go help the doctor get out of the truck and get him into my truck."

Steve rushed over to the passenger's door of the Autocar and helped Dr. Nofrio out with the donor heart.

Diesel and Paul both look at Denny's to see a firetruck, ambulance, and another police car blocking the street. Diesel and Paul look at each other. Diesel said, "Well it doesn't look like I can go that way. If I go to Forest Ave. it's going to be more than five minutes."

Joe and the waitress drove up to the right side of the Autocar and Joe tooted the antique car horn. Just as Joe stopped the car next to Paul and Diesel, Joe said, "Did you blow a hose?"

Paul said, "No, a metal fin from a car broke off, put a hole into the radiator."

Diesel was looking to the East. To the right of the car there was a throughway street that goes directly to Portland waterfront. Diesel said, "Paul, Joe can take the doctor up the back way on the other side of Barber Foods."

Paul looked to the East then turned to Joe, "Joe, can you take the doctor up the back way to Maine Med?"

Joe said, "Sure I can."

The waitress opened the passenger door and got out of the car. The doctor and Steve walked up to the driver's side of the car.

Steve said, "What's going on?"

Diesel pointed toward Denny's, "The street is blocked." Everybody looked at flashing lights.

The doctor said, “Is there another way?”

Paul looked at the doctor and Joe, “Joe will take you the back way to Maine Med.” Paul pointed toward Barber Foods.

The doctor looked at the car, then at Joe and finally at Paul.

Paul spoke, “I know what you’re thinking, you gave me the same look. Joe can and will get you there.”

Jenny walked over to the doctor, put her left hand and arm over the doctor’s left shoulder and back and said, “Don’t keep Joe waiting. When he’s got a job to do, he does it.”

Doctor Nofrio got into the passenger’s seat and Steve put the cooler onto the doctor’s lap. The Jenny closed the door, “You’re in good hands.”

Joe looked at the doctor and said, “You ready?” The doctor nodded his head and replied, “Yes.” Joe said, “Good.”

As Joe drove away, Steve looked at the license plate of the vintage Ford Phaeton car. It was 309. When they arrived at the street, Joe drove through the stop sign then turned left a little fast. The doctor put his right hand on the dashboard and a worried look came over his face. Joe shifted the transmission to a higher gear. Joe spoke, “You alright?”

The doctor said, “Yup.”

Diesel, Paul, Steve, and Jenny stood near the disabled Autocar.

Diesel spoke, “Holy shit, Joe doesn’t waste any time, does he?”

Paul said, “He never did.”

Steve looked at Paul. Paul saw Steve’s puzzled look, asked “What?”

Steve asked, “Why 309 on the license plate?”

Paul hesitated to answer, Jenny started to answer for Paul.

Then Paul spoke, "It was my wife's birthday. She loved that old car."

As they watched Joe and the doctor leave, Ralph parked his #146 Kenworth behind the trailer that was hooked to the Autocar.

Ralph walked behind and heard "never did."

Ralph said, "Oh, don't say you never did, you know you've done it at least once, twice if you liked it."

They all turned to look at Ralph,

Paul said, "Now I told you before, Ralph, that wasn't me with the sheep, it was Gary."

Jenny with a horrified look on her face said, "Oh my God, don't say anymore, I don't want to know."

Paul said as he looked at Jenny, "Maine winter nights are cold, long, and lonely after two 6-packs of beer."

"Stop it!" Jenny said as she covered her ears with her hands. Paul, Diesel, Steve, and Ralph laughed.

Then Ralph said, "Where is your passenger?"

Paul pointed toward Barber Foods where Joe and the doctor were turning left onto a small street past Barber Foods.

Joe and the doctor drove up a small hill then turned left to go up a long steep hill. Joe drove fast through several "S" curves. The doctor leaned to the left and then to the right as they went through the curves.

Joe said, "Hang on, the street will straighten out near the top of the hill." Joe continued speaking as they passed an old cemetery, "There, I told you."

Joe shifted the transmission into the next gear then saw a person walking a dog on a leash to cross the street in front of them. Joe tooted the antique horn and does not slow down.

The person grabbed the dog and ran across the street.

"He wasn't in a crosswalk."

The doctor gasped.

They could see the hospital ahead. Joe turned right, then left, and drove toward the ER entrance. Joe stopped the car in front of a City of Portland ambulance. Dr. Nofrio grabbed the door handle to open the passenger door.

The doctor looked at his watch, "Right on time."

Joe was looking at the center of the steering wheel Ford emblem. Joe said, "Do you know what Ford stands for?"

The doctor with a puzzled look got out of the antique car, "No."

"For only real drivers."

The doctor smiled, then closed the door, "Thank you."

Dr. Nofrio turned and quickly walked into the ER. He walked up to the counter at the Nurses' Station and placed the donor heart cooler on the counter in front of a nurse talking on the phone. The nurse looked at the cooler and read, "organ donor heart" on the side of the cooler. With a sigh she breathed, "Oh, shit!

She spoke into the phone, "Dr Benson needs the lab results stat. Call me back. I gotta go." She hung up the phone then spoke to Dr. Nofrio, "Can I help you?"

Dr. Nofrio said, "I'm Dr. David Nofrio from Boston Medical Center in Boston. I need to do a heart transplant for Michelle Hagerthy. She should be prepped and in the OR."

The nurse said, "Come with me, I'll take you to the Cardiac OR." Just as they start to leave the ER, the nurse stopped to tell the Portland ambulance paramedic as he was coming out of the supply room, she pointed at the phone on the counter at the nurses' station, "Stand there and answer the phone, it will be the lab results for the patient you just brought in and tell Dr. Benson the results. I'll be back." She hand-gestures and continued, "We have to go to the cardiac OR."

The paramedic looked at both the nurse and Dr. Nofrio and he said, "Ok, I'll let John know."

The nurse and Dr. Nofrio continued walking out of the ER down the hall, around a couple of corners to the elevators. The nurse pushed the button to go up.

The nurse said, "Did you come up from Boston?"

The doctor replied, "Yes." The elevator opened and they both entered the elevator and she pushed the button for the OR floor and then another button for the door to close.

The nurse said, "How did you get here so fast?"

The doctor spoke, "Oh my God, it was the most exhilarating ride of my life. It was like Mad Max mixed with a Fast and Furious on steroids!"

"Really?" the nurse asked skeptically.

The elevator has stopped at the OR floor. The doctor said, "I can say from first-hand experience, you never cut in front of a tractor trailer truck, especially an old one."

The door opened to the OR Control Desk area. Dr. Nofrio walked up to the desk and said, "I'm Dr. David Nofrio, Michelle Hagerthy is my patient. I hope she is prepped and ready for surgery."

The OR nurse, surprised, said, "We didn't expect you to be here so soon. She is over here." The nurse walked over to the patient prep area and pulled the curtain and continued speaking, "and your support staff are standing by."

Dr. Nofrio said, "Great. Hi, Michelle, I've come to see you

instead of you coming to Boston. I hate to sound like I'm in a hurry, but time is running out." He put his hand on the cooler and continued speaking, "I must change into my scrubs. I will talk to you in recovery after the surgery.

CHAPTER 13

July 3 at 3:15 PM, I-295 Congress Street Exit, Portland

Diesel, Road Boss and Ralph were still gathered around the Autocar.

Diesel disconnected Road Boss's truck from the Can Afford trailer. Ralph backed his truck under the Can Afford trailer. Paul helped with the landing gear and Diesel, after parking, walked by Ralph who was getting out of his tractor.

"Well, Paul, now we're gonna have to call Dolly Parton up and tell her she needs to sing a song about the bumper of many colors," said Diesel.

Ralph chuckled and agreed, "Yup."

"Yeah, I'll need to get the radiator fixed first," noted Paul.

"Speaking of that, what do you want to do with the beast?" Diesel asked.

"Stewart will have to tow it to Coachworks. George at Pensway will be too busy with all the dead Can Afford tractors, so I'll have to get Geno to fix the radiator," responded Paul.

"I'll try to get Chris Libby on the radio. He'll come right over," Diesel offered.

Diesel walked back to the cabover Kenworth.

Paul turned to Ralph, "Thanks a lot Ralph, for the help. The trailer is full of dunnage."

"No need to thank me, Paul, you've bailed me out more than once. Besides, we truck drivers have always helped each other out, unlike the next generation of drivers."

"Yeah, they do seem to be a bit self-centered," Paul responded.

Joe O'Hegerty drove up and tooted the horn with a smile on his face, driving up to the island ahead of Ralph's truck. Ralph and Paul walked over to Joe's door.

"Paul, your freight has been delivered on time, as always," Joe reported.

Ralph smiled and put his hand on Paul's shoulder, "Paul, just as a favor, you come out of retirement after being told Can Afford's next generation of trucks and drivers would outdo you. This trip said it all. They will never be able to fill your shoes."

Joe nodded, "Ralph's right."

"I never would have been able to do it without the old horse and all of you," Paul pointed to the Autocar.

Diesel walked up behind Paul and Ralph and reported, "Chris was dropping off a Can Afford tractor at Pensway. He said he'll be right over."

July 3 at 3:30 PM, Pensway Headquarters,

Chris unlocked the Can Afford tractor from the double-steer axle Kenworth wrecker. Chris quickly got into the driver's seat of the wrecker and drove away.

July 3 at 3:40 PM, Can Afford Warehouse, South Portland

Ralph drove away with the Can Afford trailer. Paul waved as Ralph tooted the air horn of the red W900 Kenworth.

Chris and Ralph passed each other on the Veteran Memorial Bridge. Each waved his fingers keeping both hands on the wheel. Chris drove up in front of the Autocar tractor. Joe, Paul, and Diesel were standing in front of the Phaeton behind the Autocar.

Paul walked on the left side of the Autocar to meet Chris at the back of the wrecker. Diesel and Joe walked side-by-side behind Paul.

"Watch Chris's face when he gets a look at Paul's bumper," Diesel warned.

Just then Chris made it to the back of the wrecker.

"Holy shit! How many cars did you destroy?"

Diesel chuckled. Joe smiled. Paul answered, "Yeah, well you know, I never kept count, but it was a lot."

"You'll have to tell all about it later. I've got a lot of Can Afford tractors to tow back to Pensway," Chris laughed.

Chris and Paul hooked the tow truck to the Autocar.

Steve returned from walking Jenny to Maine Med.

Paul spoke, "How's things going at Maine Med?"

"The doctor was in surgery with Michelle and Jenny was with Albert's kids in the lounge area of recovery.

Paul said, "Good. I'm going with Chris to Coach Works then Joe and I are going back to O'Hegerty. Hopefully Albert will be back in South Portland."

Yeah, Albert and Gonzo were coming into Pensway's yard when I left to come here," Chris said.

Paul said, "Chris, are you all good with dropping off at Geno's Shop?"

"Yes."

Steve said, "I'll help Chris."

Paul thanked them both. Paul turned to Diesel, "I'll catch up with you later."

"Yeah, I'm going back to the warehouse, I'm sure they're still in desperate need of help."

Paul turned back to Joe, "Joe, are you ready?"

"As ready as I'll ever be."

"Good, let's go." Paul and Joe walked over to the Phaeton, Paul drove, with Joe as his passenger, toward the Veteran Memorial's Bridge. Chris and Steve followed.

Diesel, Paul, and Joe drove the backway to the warehouse. Just as Paul and Joe made it to the intersection of Can Afford's Warehouse Main Gate, Albert with the W900 day cab was leaving the warehouse Main Gate.

Joe said, "There's Albert now. Talk about timing."

Paul waved to Albert. Paul and Joe followed Albert. Albert turned right into Pensway's yard and parked the W900 tractor. Paul drove past the Pensway yard then turned right into the O'Hegerty' Office driveway then parked in the little parking lot behind the office.

Paul and Joe got out and walked into the drivers' room. Mark O'Hegerty and Bob Tyghman were talking to Gonzo and Troy at the table. Troy got up from the table and gave a piece of paper to Donald at the dispatch window. He had compiled a list of trailer numbers that were loaded and needed to be returned to the Maine Can Afford warehouse and the New York warehouse. Everybody stopped talking when Joe and Paul entered the drivers' room.

Gonzo said, "Hey, it's Mad Max himself." Mark and Bob both stood and shook Paul's hand.

Mark said, "Ralph told us about your truck, how bad is it?"

"It's going to need another radiator, that should be it," Paul answered.

"Really?" Mark questioned.

"Well, maybe a front-end alignment and some front tires. I did kinda run over and through a few abandoned cars."

They all laughed a little.

Then Albert walked into the driver's room, and everybody stopped talking. Albert put his trip sheets in the dispatch window, then quickly walked to the bathroom. A few minutes later Albert came out drying his hands with a paper towel. Paul was now standing near the bathroom door.

Albert hesitated but asked Paul, "Did you make it?"

"Within a mile, then Joe came along to save the day."

Paul pointed at Joe and continued, "Dr. Nofrio is in surgery with Michelle. Jenny is with Marc and Felicia waiting in Recovery. I need to get you over there."

Joe was standing by the dispatch window, Albert said, "Thank you."

Joe smiled, Paul went outside then Joe spoke, "You need to go, Paul will leave without you."

Albert quickly followed Paul as Paul was getting into the Phaeton. Albert stopped for a second then got in the passenger's side door.

"What happened to your pick-up?" Albert asked.

"I left it at home."

Paul and Albert drove out O'Hegerty driveway following two antique tractors pulling Can Afford trailers.

"Who got those old trucks to haul Can Afford trailers?" Albert asked.

"Well, Kenny Hewey came by Rudy's this morning asking

for help. Diesel and I were headed to Owl's Head Museum for the annual antique truck show so we told Kenny we were meeting up with some friends and their antique trucks at Sebago Brewing Restaurant and we would ask."

Paul paused as he stopped at a 4-way traffic light intersection. When he continued driving Albert asked, "What happened to your truck?"

"Oh, some dumbass drove in front of me at the 295 toll booth. The car had one of those air scoop fins on the trunk, so when I rear ended him the fin broke off and went through the radiator of the truck. I got to the off ramp by Denny's when the engine shut down."

Albert said, "Where is it now?"

Paul said, "It's at Coach Works, Geno will fix it."

"Yeah, he will," Albert nodded.

Paul and Albert arrived at Maine Medical Center. Paul parked in the parking lot across the street from the ER. They both quickly walked into the main entrance and reached the OR Recovery Nurses' Station.

Albert asked to the nurse, "My wife, Michelle Hagerthy, is she still in surgery?"

The nurse was looking through some patient charts and she jumped and looked up at Albert and Paul, "Ah, yes, she is."

Albert said, "My son and daughter are here. Do you know where they are?"

The nurse put down the charts, "Oh, yes, follow me."

The nurse started to walk across to a set of double doors when Albert asked, "How much longer should the surgery last?"

The nurse continued through the double doors and to a

lounge area with a television. Albert and Paul followed her into the lounge area. Felicia looked up at Albert then jumped up from the chair and hugged her father. Kayla stood beside Felicia and Albert reached out to hug her. Jenny stood and grabbed Paul's hand then gave him a half a hug and a kiss on the cheek.

Marc looked up and stood. The nurse spoke carefully, "If everything goes well it will be a couple more hours."

Albert said, "Thank you."

The nurse left.

Marc said, "I did tell Aunt Sue to take care of the dogs before we left home."

Albert said, "Good, I can't call to ask."

Then Albert looked at the television and Marc was watching X-Men Apocalypse. Albert looked with a puzzled look on his face and said, "How are you watching television?"

Marc said, "I brought some DVDs from home."

Albert said, "Oh." He hesitated as he watched the movie. Albert continued speaking, "What movie was that?"

Marc spoke, "X-Men Apocalypse."

Albert exhaled with a huff, "Really, Marc?"

"What? It's a great movie."

Albert looked over to Paul and Jenny, then just shook his head.

Felicia and Kayla sat down. Jenny walked over and hugged Albert, "Everything is going to be alright."

"Yeah," Albert replied with a yawn.

Jenny saw Albert's yawn then asked, "When was the last time you had something to eat?"

Albert said, "I had two oatmeal cookies on my way up from Boston the second time."

"What? You need to eat! Let's go to the cafeteria. Come on, Paul, you need to eat too."

Jenny grabbed Albert by his right arm to turn him to leave the lounge area, then she stopped and turned to speak to Felicia, "Felicia, I'm taking your father and Paul to get something to eat at the cafeteria."

Felicia replied, "Ok, I'll come get you if anything comes up."

"We won't be that long," Albert said over his shoulder as all three of them walked away toward the cafeteria.

During the walk Albert asked Paul, "How did you end up bringing Dr. Nofrio to Maine Med?" Paul started telling Albert and Jenny about the CB Radio call from Diesel then how he bob-tailed to Durty Nellie's in Boston and picked up the doctor. Then related how he crushed a taxicab and drove north on Route 1 South from the Tobin Bridge to the Lynnfield Tunnel. He told both of them how a Saugus cop chased them and how he lost the cop by leaving Route 1.

Jenny asked, "How was the doctor reacting through all of this?"

Paul chuckled, "Yeah, he was freaked out at first. But by the time we made it through to 95 in Peabody, he became quite the co-pilot." As they talked, they filled their trays with food and made it to the cash register in the cafeteria. About halfway through eating Paul said, "I think what really freaked the doctor out the most was when we were coming by the Saco exit and I told him we were doing 105 mph."

Jenny just shook her head and Albert sat with his eyes open wide and spoke, "Wow, it would me too!"

They finished eating then started walking back to the

lounge area. Just before the doorway to Recovery, Albert spoke, "Well, the doctor can say now that ride with you was most definitely the ride of a lifetime."

The nurse at the Recovery Nurses' Station saw Albert, Paul, and Jenny walk through the door. She stood up, "Mr. Hagerthy." Albert, Paul, and Jenny stopped and looked at the nurse.

Albert said, "You don't have to call me mister, Albert is fine."

The nurse said, "Good news, the surgery went well. The donor heart is beating on its own."

Albert smiled and signed with relief.

Jenny, "Thank you, Jesus!" with a big smile on her face she hugged Paul and kissed his cheek. She continued, "And, thank you, Paul."

Paul smiled.

Albert asked, "When can I see her?"

The nurse said, "Dr. Nofrio was finishing up, he'll be out soon to tell you everything."

Albert nodded and turned to Paul and hugged him. "Thank you," Albert said with a big smile.

Jenny went into the lounge and told Felicia, Kayla, and Marc the good news. They all jumped up for joy, then Felicia ran to Albert and gave him a bear hug. They both smiled.

Felicia said, "When do we get to see mom?"

Albert said, "Dr. Nofrio will be out shortly to tell us everything."

Then Marc hugged Albert, "Thank God."

Albert said, "Yeah, Him too!" Then they all walked back to the lounge area to sit and wait for Dr. Nofrio to come out.

Kayla spoke, "I was online the other day reading about recipients of other people's organs. It said the recipient sometimes has characteristics of the donor, especially if it was a heart."

Marc said, "Dad, you better hope the donor was a female or you're in trouble." Albert looked at Marc with disgust.

Paul and Jenny looked at each other. Paul and Jenny grinned at the joke.

Marc said, "I'm just sayin'." Then there was a moment of silence.

Then the nurse came into the lounge, "Dr. Nofrio wants you to know the operation is complete and he will be out in a couple of minutes."

Albert got up quickly as the nurse was speaking, and said, "Good," still concerned. "Thank you," he nodded.

The nurse left the lounge area and Albert started to pace around the lounge area. The door from the OR opened and Dr. Nofrio walked toward where Albert was standing. Albert walked up to Dr. Nofrio, his eyes wide open and his forehead wrinkled with worry.

Dr. Nofrio reached out to shake Albert's hand, "Everything went well, she is still sedated. It will be best that we keep her sedated for at least the next 10 to 18 hours. Then we will wake her up and take her off the ventilator. She will have a sore throat. We'll be doing blood work periodically to check her white blood cell count to ensure that the heart is working and that Michelle's body is accepting the heart.

Albert nodded.

Felicia and Kayla stood up beside Albert as the doctor was talking to Albert.

Felicia asked Dr. Nofrio, "What do you know about the donor?"

Dr. Nofrio replied, "She was a Hispanic marathon runner, in her early thirties, on life support and due to a power outage, the life support shut down and did not get restarted in time."

Felicia asked another question, "Why was she on life support?"

Dr. Nofrio replied, "She was on her morning run and was struck by a car that drove up onto the sidewalk where she was running."

Felicia and Kayla look at each other, Felicia is stunned.

Kayla spoke, "Oh my God," then hesitated, "Did she see the car coming at her?"

Dr. Nofrio answered, "I don't know. I heard some of the nurses talking about the driver of the car. He was texting while driving."

Dr. Nofrio continued speaking, looking at Albert, "I'm going to the cafeteria for something to eat. When I come back, we'll go see Michelle, ok?"

Albert said, "Yeah, go, you deserve a break." Albert reached out and shook the doctor's hand, "Thank you."

Dr. Nofrio turned to leave and looked at Paul sitting with Jenny. He pointed at Paul, "There's the hero that truly made this all possible."

Paul smiled.

Dr. Nofrio left and went to the cafeteria. Jenny grabbed Paul's hand, "You really are a hero."

Paul replied, "I couldn't have done it without the old beast."

Felicia spoke to Albert, "Mom is going to feel like a new person with a marathon runner's heart."

"Yeah, I'm pretty sure she won't want to do any running anytime soon."

Felicia said, "No, but you know what I mean."

Albert spoke, "Yup."

CHAPTER 14

July 4 Recovery Room, Maine Medical Center, Portland, Maine

Michelle was lying, still asleep, with an oxygen tube going up both nostrils, a ventilator in her mouth. Wires sprouted from under the blanket, hooked up to a cardiac monitor and several IV tubes were hooked up to IV pumps. A nurse entered Michelle's room with the phlebotomist. The phlebotomist drew a tube of blood from Michelle then left. The nurse checked the cardiac monitor then the leads. She took Michelle's temperature then blood pressure. As the nurse checked the readings, she wrote down the information on Michelle's chart. The nurse checked all chest bandages then straightened out the blankets by Michelle's shoulders, then the nurse left the room.

Michelle was lying still. Her pupils moved under her eyelids. The pupils moved left to right, and her eyelids started to squint and relax.

Dr. Nofrio, the same nurse, and Albert walked into the room. Albert was dressed in OR scrubs.

Dr. Nofrio said "Now I know it looks really bad with all the equipment, wires and IV tubes. I assure you it is not as bad as it looks, but all of it will help her recover faster. I will be staying here in the hospital. The nurses will keep me informed of Michelle's recovery. It has been a very long day, so I need to get some sleep. You, yourself, look like you need to get some sleep. So go home, then come back in the morning. Then we will wake her up."

Albert replied "Yes, I've been to Boston twice today. The last trip coming back here was the longest."

Doctor Nofrio agreed, nodding his head, "My trip up here was one I will never forget."

Albert holds Michelle's hand and tells her "I love you, I will be back in the morning with Turkey one and two plus Kayla."

Albert and Doctor Nofrio started to walk out.

Doctor Nofrio stopped "I have to talk to the nurse, so I will see you tomorrow morning."

Albert nodded "Thank you again for all you have done."

Doctor Nofrio smiled, then Albert left. Just as Albert arrived in the waiting room, Felicia jumped up and asked, "How was she?"

"She was sleeping. They have her sedated. We will come back tomorrow morning, Doctor Nofrio said your mother needs to rest for at least ten to eighteen hours. So, let's go home and come back first thing in the morning."

They all left the hospital, walked to the parking lot across the street and got into Felicia's Ford Explorer. Felicia drove everyone home. When they arrived, Albert started the generator so they all could take a shower and keep the refrigerator and the freezer cold. The next morning everyone got up, ate breakfast, got dressed, piled into Felicia's Explorer and headed to the hospital.

They all are tired and anxious. Felicia worriedly asked, "OK, Dad, did Doctor Nofrio say anything about a limit of how many people can be in the room when Mom wakes up?"

"No, he didn't say. The ICU room was not very big, so I'm sure there is a limit."

Felicia demanded, "I want to be there when she wakes up,"

In a softer tone, Kayla said, "Me too, she is my second Mom."

Marc looked at both of them and just shook his head.

Albert said, "I will ask the Doctor, you may have to put on OR scrubs like I did yesterday."

Felicia and Kayla looked at each other and say together "We don't care."

Marc said, "What about me?"

Felicia quickly replied "No! We come first. You're just a peasant, you'll have to wait."

Marc huffs.

Albert said, "Alright, let's wait till we get there and find out from Doctor Nofrio. To save you all the cat and dog fight."

On their way back to the hospital, they passed three Can Afford tractors parked on the side of the route 295 highway. Albert looked at the tractors and shook his head. "I'm glad the truck I drove doesn't have a computer in it."

They made it to Portland and rode through the city streets. City workers are putting up temporary Stop signs at some street intersections where the traffic lights no longer work. They arrived at the hospital parking lot, then they nearly jogged to get into the hospital. Once inside, Albert checked with patient registration and security to let them know where they were headed. Now they continued to Cardiac ICU.

As they approach the nurses' station, Doctor Nofrio was

looking over Michelle's overnight chart and talking to the head nurse of ICU. Doctor Nofrio and the nurse look at Albert and the kids come into the waiting room area. He told her that he needed two lab test results stat.

Dr. Nofrio finished at the nurses' station and walked over to Albert near the doorway of the waiting room.

Dr. Nofrio said, "Well, you made it back. Did you get much sleep?"

"Yes," Albert nodded.

Doctor Nofrio reported, "Good, we must wait for some lab results to come back. So, it may be about thirty minutes.

Albert nodded and asked "Ok, oh the kids want to know if they can be there when Michelle wakes up."

Doctor Nofrio replied "I don't have a problem with them being there. But I don't make the rules for this hospital. I will see what I can do. Michelle is in a small room, so there may be only room enough for one other person. Again, I will talk with the nurse supervisor."

Albert nodded his head and said, "I'll tell the girls to cross their fingers."

Just then Paul and Jenny walked into the waiting room.

Doctor Nofrio looked at them and smiled, "WOW the gang's all here"

Paul said, "That's right we wouldn't miss this for the world," as Jenny nodded.

Doctor Nofrio said "I'm going to check on the lab results. I'll be back."

Both Paul and Jenny have concerned looked on their faces and asked at the same time, "What's going on?"

Albert said "Doctor Nofrio is very thorough, he is waiting

for some lab work results. He wants to make sure everything is perfect."

Jenny said "Good" then she looked at the kids and stepped toward them and asked, "How are you holding out?"

Felicia and Kayla replied, "We can't wait to see her."

Then Marc said "Me too"

Paul said to Albert, "I spoke with Donald yesterday late afternoon."

Albert asked, "What did he say?"

Paul said, "Ok and yes."

Albert asked, "What did you say to him?"

Paul said, "I simply told him, he was to give all the time you need. Plus, he was to pay you for it. Yes, he was going to say something. But then I stood up and all he said was OK, OK."

Albert laughed a little, "Well, you are a lot bigger than he is. Thank you."

Dr. Nofrio returned, "Good news, the lab results are very good. So, we can go in and wake her up."

Felicia and Kayla responded, "YAY."

Doctor Nofrio said, "I asked the Nurse Supervisor about the Hospital Visitation policy. She said due to everything involved, and I had to agree, just one visitor at first."

Felicia said, "Damn it"

Doctor Nofrio quickly replied, "But, she did say you can come into ICU. You will be able to see your mother wake up through the glass. The room unit is small, I know that's not what you wanted but, you can see her, and she will be able to see you."

Felicia said with a sigh, "ok" Kayla nodded her head to agree.

Doctor Nofrio said, “So, let me talk to the nurse assisting me just to make sure we have everything we need, and I’ll be right back.”

Doctor Nofrio walked back to the nurse’s station.

Marc said “So, can I go into the ICU also?”

Albert said, “He said you could, but you all will be quiet and not in the way. Understand?”

All three answer, “Yes.”

Doctor Nofrio comes back and said, “We are all set. Let’s get started.

Felicia and Kayla quickly stood up, then Marc stood.

Then Felicia went to push Marc and she said, “We’re first.”

Marc said, “Dad just said we all can go.”

Albert quickly turned around and said very firmly “Quit the SHIT RIGHT NOW or NO ONE GOES IN.” All three stopped with shocked looks on their faces.

Marc got behind Kayla with Felicia ahead of her. They all walked in line as they went through the doors of ICU. The nurse opened the glass door to let Albert in. Albert entered and the nurse closed the sliding door. Felicia, Kayla, and Marc stood just outside the glass door looking at Michelle with a little bit of shock on their faces. They saw all the equipment hooked up to Michelle.

The doctor checked Michelle’s chart then checked her heartbeat with a stethoscope. Dr. Nofrio removed the stethoscope from his ears then looked at Albert. Dr. Nofrio said, “Well, let’s get to it and wake her up from whatever she’s dreaming about.”

They both look at Michelle’s eyelids moving. Dr. Nofrio started the wake-up process. A couple of minutes go by as Albert, the doctor, and the nurse watch Michelle's facial expressions get more theatrical. Then Michelle's head turned to the left then to the right. She started to mumble words, "Move... look...out...the train."

Now Michelle's eyes open and Albert grabbed her hand. Albert looked at Michelle's face then he whispered, "Michelle."

Michelle's eyes opened wide, and she looked at Albert.

Albert said "It's ok, there's no train. You're at Maine Med, you have had a heart transplant. You are safe, there are no trains here."

Then Michelle looked at Doctor Nofrio and the nurse. Then looked at her arms with the IV's and the heart monitor screen on her left. Felicia knocked on the glass, Michelle quickly looked up to see Felicia, Kayla, and Marc smiling and waving at her. Michelle smiled a little and gave a half of a wave.

Doctor Nofrio said "Michelle, your surgery went very well. We will be doing a lot of lab testing and heart monitoring on you for the next few days. Are you feeling any pain and where?"

Michelle said, "I'm hungry, my mouth is a little dry." Doctor Nofrio said "Well, we will get you some easy food to digest and some water," as he was looking at Michelle then the nurse. The nurse left the room to get some food and water.

Albert said "Michelle, what were you dreaming about a train for?" Michelle said, "This loud train horn was going off then there was a lot of crashing."

Doctor Nofrio was touching the Heart monitoring screen, then he stopped suddenly with his eyes wide open. As he looked at Michelle and said, "Really."

Then Michelle said, "Yeah, and a loud roar from an engine."

Doctor Nofrio has a perplexed look on his face in disbelief. Now the nurse returned with some food and water. Doctor Nofrio said “Oh good, now eat slowly. I have to speak with the cardiologists here about you and what they need to do. I do have other patients like you in Boston. So, I need to go back to Boston in the next couple of days. I’ll be back in an hour or so.”

Michelle was looking at the food and Albert said “Ok, thank you for all of what you have done.”

Doctor Nofrio smiled and shook Albert’s right hand and said, “You’re very welcome.” then left the room.

Playlist

When I was writing this book, I decided that I needed a sound track. My dream would be to use the following songs; if this were to be made into a film.

•

3009 Coach White Mini Van
License Plate 309 AKA (Always Kicking Ass)
Grateful Dead - "Truckin"
Dick Curless - "Big Wheel Cannonball"
SailCat - "Motorcycle Mama"
David Allen Coe - "You Never Even Call Me by My Name"
Blues Album
Badlands
Truffle Under Foot
Bachman Turner Overdrive - "Roll on Down the Highway" (1975)
LeAnne Rimes - "How Do I Live" (1997)
LeAnne Rimes - "Change of Your Heart" (1987) or
(Change of Heart, Cyndi Lauper, David Sanborn?)
Genesis - "Land of Confusion" (1987)
Mindy McCready - "Ten Thousand Angels"
Reba McEntire - "I know How He Feels"
Tim McGraw - "Not a moment Too Soon"
Lonestar- "Smile"
AC/DC - "Thunderstruck"
Billy Joel - "She's Got a Way"
A-Ha - "Take on Me"
Aerosmith - "Dream On"
Madonna - "Live to Tell" (1986)

AC/DC - "Back in Black" (1981)
AC/DC - "Highway to Hell"
Air Supply - "Every Woman in the World"
Terri Gibbs - "Somebody's Knockin'"
Red Sovine - "Giddy Up, Go" (Paul leaving the barn)
Bon Jovi - "Because We Can"
Aerosmith - "Living on the Edge"
George Strait - "I Cross My Heart"
Eddie Rabbit - "Driving My Life Away"
George Jones - "Who's Gonna Fill Their Shoes"
Heartland Express Truck - needs to be in line for Maine
Dry Van #2726
Pottle's Transport Trailer
7 Million People Move America Forward - One is Driving This Truck

www.ingramcontent.com/pod-product-compliance
Ingram Content Group UK Ltd.
Pitfield, Milton Keynes, MK11 3LW, UK
UKHW021649190726
13853UKWH00001B/150